Cecilia Tan

THE HOT STREAK

A Baseball Romance

THE HOT STREAK

A BASEBALL ROMANCE

by Cecilia Tan

For more information contact:
Riverdale Avenue Books
5676 Riverdale Avenue
Riverdale, NY 10471
www.riverdaleavebooks.com
Cover by Scott Carpenter

Digital ISBN 978-1-62601-096-3
Print ISBN 978-1-62601-097-0

Previously published in 2009, Ravenous Romance.
First RAB Edition 2014.

Riverdale Avenue Books would like to thank you for reading this copy of The Hot Streak by gifting you one free book from each imprint, which you can download at the link provided:
https://preview.mailerlite.io/preview/1098983/sites/136486432257607665/0kJ9TD

If you are interested in being in our ARC reader/reviewer program, you can sign up here. Reviews are the life blood of the independent author and publisher and every single one counts to getting books into the hands of the right readers.

What They are Saying about **THE HOT STREAK**

"*The Hot Streak* is a sweet, enjoyable quick read. The chemistry, sexual tension, lust was off the charts, and I really got into their relationship."

—BJ's Book Blog

"Tyler was a great lead, funny, caring, and enthusiastic about everything. He was a bit like an overgrown Labrador puppy, words spilling out of his mouth without thought, impulse buys and actions... and yet you can't help liking him."

—Jeannie Zelos Book Reviews

"I thought Tyler and Casey were an excellent pair—and found her attempt to follow the team for his sake endearing! All in all? A great, quick read for fans of baseball!"

—For Love and Books

"This hot novel keeps you on your toes with its spicy scenes and drama. Yet what I loved most about it was Tyler with his happy-go-lucky look on life and infectious personality!"

—From Me to You Book Reviews

"I am a huge baseball fan which drew me to this novel in the first place. I instantly fell in love with Casey and Tyler. I also love the fact that the story wasn't like every other romance novel where the lead male character knew he was broken and wanted a woman to help fix him. I also love how Tan used a lot of baseball terms and tied in so much of the game into the book!"

—Adventure in Bookland

"*The Hot Streak* is an interesting take on loving someone who is in the limelight. I enjoyed the book and found it to be an entertaining read."

—Coffee Time Romance

CHAPTER ONE

Casey felt like a little girl on her way to the circus. That was the only thing she could think of to compare it to, as she rode the packed train toward the ballpark. There was a kind of excitement in the crowd, and as she elbowed her way out of the car with the rest of the passengers, she couldn't help but be caught up in it.

She wasn't completely sure which way to go, but surrounded by people in Robins hats and jerseys and T-shirts, she figured all she had to do was go with the flow. The river of brightly clad people buoyed her along toward the stadium. The summer breeze blew warm off Boston Harbor while the sun set somewhere behind the skyline. The glow of stadium lights ahead and the tinny sound of music from the PA system seemed to beckon the crowd. People chattered excitedly all around her, and she caught the sound of a familiar name in it.

Hammond, Tyler Hammond.

The two women directly in front of her were talking about the very guy who had invited Casey to this game.

"What? It's Hammond starting? I thought it was Gutierrez

on the mound tonight." The woman was in her forties, Casey guessed, blond, with overlong nails and too many rings. She reminded Casey of her Aunt Mary.

"That was last night," her friend replied. "Why do you think I'm wearing my Tyler Hammond jersey? Hello?" The other woman slid her long, dark hair aside, and pointed at her back to emphasize the point. Casey blinked. Right there, it said *Hammond,* with a large number thirteen sewn in black satin on the orange-red cloth.

She had the urge to ask them, *What's he like? Is he a decent guy? I met him today at work and I have no clue what I'm doing here...*

But as the crowd grew thicker closer to the park, she lost sight of them. Time to figure out where to pick up the tickets. The stadium was only a few years old, a gleaming jewel on the waterfront, built to entice a National League team to Boston and, so said the cynical business columnists, to eat into the huge market of baseball fans the Red Sox had formerly monopolized. It had been big news at the time, but Casey hadn't paid much attention in recent years and she'd never been to the ballpark before. She eventually found the window labeled "Team/Family/VIP"—a handwritten sign taped on the inside of the glass. Behind it stood a gray-haired woman wearing a red polo shirt with the Robins logo embroidered on it.

"Last name?" she barked at Casey through the grill.

"Branigan," Casey answered. "Tyler Hammond said he left me..."

"Branigan," the woman repeated. "Cassie?"

"Casey," she corrected, more annoyed at having been cut off than at the woman getting her name wrong.

"Whatever. ID, please?"

Casey slipped her driver's license into the little metal well under the window, and the woman slid it back along with a ticket. "Enjoy the game. *Next!*"

Casey put her license back into her wallet, feeling a bit like she was at the airport as she prepared to go through security. Were they going to want to see it again? They were searching people's bags up ahead. But all she had was her little handbag, too small even to hold a single bottle of smuggled beer in it, much less a weapon of mass destruction. The guard just gave it a cursory glance and waved her through.

She made her way through the brick and concrete building, making her way along wide walkways edged with vending stalls selling popcorn and hot dogs; it smelled like the circus, too. A man selling bags of cotton candy lined up on a long pole edged past her and up a ramp toward the seats. She examined the numbers posted above the ramp and walked on further, looking for hers.

She came to what looked to be the right ramp and headed up a narrow concrete tunnel toward the bright lights.

Suddenly she was standing in the bowl of the stadium, the field huge and green in front of her. Players were spread out over the grass and for a moment she panicked, thinking she was late, but she quickly realized they weren't playing yet. They were stretching and practicing their moves. She stared, the way one would if the actors in a Broadway play were wandering around on the stage before a show. But then an usher noticed her lost look and steered her to a seat about ten rows back from the field.

The whole section was empty; no one else near her had shown up yet. She bought a program from a passing vendor so she would have something to read while waiting, but she

THE HOT STREAK

ended up looking around. *I'm really not supposed to be here,* she thought, and it seemed surreal to be sitting under bright lights in the open air.

She was supposed to be at a party right then. A "work" party being thrown by one of her regular clients, a launch party for the new "look" for their magazine, and she supposed she should have gone to be supportive and to network. But open-bar-and-*crudite* just didn't have the appeal it once did. *I never promised I'd go,* she rationalized. It wasn't as if she got paid to spend non-work hours attending that sort of thing, either. *Well, thank you, Tyler Hammond, for getting me away from that for a night.* She looked for him on the field, but didn't see him among the players there. Men raked the dirt and just a few Robins were off to one side playing catch and doing little sprints. She felt a thrill of excitement when she thought she caught sight of him—but no, that was someone else.

They'd met earlier in the day, when she was helping to set up a photo shoot for another magazine her company worked for. There had been two athletes involved, Tyler and another whose name Casey had forgotten now. The photographer had been aiming for some high-concept image with Tyler in a suit of armor, but Casey hadn't paid much attention to the photographer. Not once Tyler had started to pay attention to her.

Casey generally did not flirt at work. Working in a production bureau normally did not bring her into contact with many flirt-worthy subjects, anyway. And today, she had not flirted either. It was all Tyler. If he hadn't been so persistent, she probably would have just laughed him off and not taken him up on the offer of the free ticket.

She sat up straighter suddenly; there he was.

He hopped up the dugout steps and started walking across

the grass. With him went a player carrying a large bag, and an older man Casey guessed must be a coach. They were fifty yards away at least, and Tyler was wearing a hat, but she was sure it was him.

Well, that and the fact that his jersey said *Hammond* on the back with a number thirteen, just like that woman's.

The other player walking with him had *Madison* on his back. Casey wondered how players felt about women wearing clothes with their names on them. Was it sort of weird? Would Tyler expect his girlfriend or wife to wear a *Hammond* jersey?

Casey shook her head. *I can't believe I'm thinking about stuff like that.* He was a sweet guy, but it wasn't as if she expected anything to come of it. He had been nice to leave the ticket and it was a great excuse to get away from a boring work function and do something different for once. Casey watched the little trio open a gate in the far wall in the outfield and disappear through it. She was just wondering where they had gone when a woman took the seat next to her.

She was alone, not wearing any team colors, her hair a perfect auburn; her jewelry looked expensive. The woman glanced at Casey, then took a magazine out of her shoulder bag and began to read as if she were waiting for a bus rather than a baseball game.

The words were out of Casey's mouth almost before she realized it. "Oh my goodness, I worked on that magazine." It was the fashionable home publication whose party she was skipping out on, as if Fate were trying to remind her about it.

The woman looked up. "Oh?"

"Yes. I did some independent art direction for them. I work at a production bureau here in town...sorry, that might sound like Greek. I helped with their photography and layout." Casey held out her hand. "Casey Branigan."

"Pleased to meet you," the woman said, shaking her hand hard. "I'm Missy Madison."

Something about the way she said it made it sound like she expected Casey to recognize it. Casey hesitated, eyebrow raised, as if trying to place it, and the woman went on. "Mad Dog's wife."

Madison, she had said. "Oh, the fellow I saw walking with Tyler?"

Her smile warmed suddenly, seemed more genuine. "You're here with Tyler?"

"Well, not *with*..." Casey started, then stopped. "I mean, he was nice enough to give me a ticket. I'm not, I mean..."

Missy smiled and patted Casey on the arm. "He's fun, Tyler is," she said and her smile turned knowing.

Casey didn't know what to say to that, so she just smiled in return while wondering what she was getting herself into.

The stands filled up around them and while listening to the people talking in the rows nearby, Casey eventually figured out that everyone in the section was a friend or the family of someone on the team. The only ones who weren't relatives or significant others were the two guys sitting right behind her, who seemed to be some kind of executives in the company that ran the ice cream concessions at the stadium, at least as far as she could tell from eavesdropping on them. Missy introduced her to a few of the other women, and Casey was making small talk with them when the crowd started to cheer and holler.

Out on the field, Tyler and Mad Dog and the guy who was presumably a coach were walking back toward the dugout from the outfield. None of the other players was on the field now, just some workmen raking the dirt and watering it down. The three of them were taking their time crossing the grass, and more and more of the crowd began to cheer as they noticed them, turning their walk into a kind of parade.

A woman came running down the aisle, her camera in hand. "Tyler, I love you!" she shouted, waving, then taking a flurry of pictures as he waved in their general direction and disappeared down the dugout steps.

It was the woman Casey had seen earlier, in the Hammond jersey. She ran excitedly back up the aisle. Casey turned around to see her friend, giving her a thumbs-up.

Missy put a hand on her wrist. "Don't let it bother you. If it does, don't get involved," she said in a low voice. She turned back to her magazine then, as if she hadn't just given Casey a fairly personal piece of advice.

She didn't have long to mull it over before the action began on the field again. The Robins emerged, along with their mascot who looked like a giant stuffed animal, all plush. The big stuffie proceeded to gambol atop the dugout while the players began to warm up.

Tyler's face looked far more serious than earlier. He had pushed his cap down low over his eyes, and, well, it barely looked like him. He stood on the little hill in the middle of the field like a statue on a pedestal, then all of a sudden he kicked his leg up like an Alvin Ailey dancer, and made a sort of pinwheel of arms and legs, out of which came the ball. Even with the pumped-up music playing, Casey could hear the ball hit the catcher's glove.

"Does it always sound like that?" she asked Missy.

"Does what always sound like what?"

"Never mind." Obviously was normal for it to smack so loudly. "It sounds like he throws hard."

She smiled. "Honey, nobody throws harder than 'The Hammer.'"

"Is that what they call him?"

Missy nodded. "That and the 'Big Ham,' 'Ham and Cheese...'"

"Wait, 'Ham and *Cheese*?'"

"They call a fastball 'hard cheese,' and any guy with a name that starts with H-A-M..." She shrugged. "Ballplayers aren't exactly always geniuses when it comes to nicknames."

So spoke the wife of a man they called "Mad Dog." Casey nodded.

People around them were starting to get to their feet and Casey wondered why. It reminded her of being in church as a child and trying to figure out how the adults all knew when to stand up. The announcement that came over the PA system soon cleared up the confusion, though, as a voice asked everyone to rise for the National Anthem.

The players on the field grouped together a bit. The three outfielders stood shoulder to shoulder, the infielders on each side, too. Tyler stood on the mound alone, though, with his cap over his heart and his head bowed so his chin touched his chest. He looked solemn. Lonely. Determined. Not at all like the happy-go-lucky guy who had flirted with her all afternoon.

Casey realized she was probably reading too much into things, but she couldn't help the feeling that she was there to see a play. A very odd play, acted out in pantomime and interpretive dance, where each movement represented something.

And it was certainly dramatic. Tyler struck out the first three batters for the other team, the crowd's cheers getting louder on each one. The Robins managed to get a runner home in the next inning, but that was it, and for a couple of innings the whole place was tense, like they were waiting for a storm to break. Casey didn't need to know anything about baseball to realize that being ahead by only one was precarious.

Then in the sixth, the pantomime played out in a way that even Casey could see. The other team got a few men on, but they hadn't scored yet and there were two outs. The batter who came to the plate was huge. He could have been cast as a villain in a James Bond movie; that was how big and menacing he was as he walked from the sidelines, waving his bat.

Strike him out, Tyler, come on, she thought.

But his first pitch hit the big palooka on the shoulder. The guy went down to one knee for a second, then sprang up, more enraged than injured, just like if Bond had punched him in the face and he just kept coming. The batter was shouting, Tyler was shouting back. The umpire and Mad Dog got between them, everyone walking gradually toward first base as all four of them were shouting now. Mad Dog was chest to chest with Tyler, holding him back from charging the guy. A Robins coach came running over, then another one came out of the dugout, there was much gesticulation...

The next thing Casey knew, there was something of a scrum happening, and coaches and other players were pulling Tyler and the other guy apart, and a lot of players had run onto the field who didn't seem to be doing anything helpful but staring.

Then everyone went back to their places except for one coach and one umpire, who argued for a while. Then the coach waved to the outfield and went back down into the dugout. Tyler was nowhere to be seen. "What just happened?" Casey asked Missy.

"Looks like Tyler got ejected from the game. Campbell, too, from the looks of it." She pointed to a skinny guy now at first base, stretching his legs. And a pitcher came through the doorway in the fence and jogged to the mound.

The poor kid was getting booed. "Okay, and isn't that guy on our team? Why are people booing?"

"Well..." Missy looked around. "They are booing the umpire for tossing Tyler, but the new pitcher, his name's Javier, and he's not been doing well lately. And the bases are loaded and he has only a one-run lead. So there's no margin for error."

Casey crossed her arms. That didn't seem quite right. "Yeah, but...shouldn't they be cheering to try to give him some encouragement? I mean, if you destroy the guy's confidence, how's he supposed to do well for you?"

Missy laughed. "You should have been a psychologist. A crowd isn't like a rational person. A crowd sees something they like, they cheer. Something they don't like, they boo. It's pretty simple. The guys learn not to take it personally."

Casey tried to imagine thousands of people booing her and not taking it personally. She didn't manage it.

On the other hand, the next batter hit the ball straight up, Mad Dog caught it when it came down, and then there were huge cheers for Javier. "I see what you mean."

Things went on from there, and in the next inning, Mad Dog hit a home run to make it two to nothing, which made the lead and the crowd more comfortable, and Casey started thinking about heading home. The ice cream guys had already left, so it seemed like it was an acceptable thing to do. She had work in the morning, after all, and it was nine thirty already, and the player she had come to see was out of the game. She was just going to turn to Missy to say goodbye and thanks, when a warm hand on her shoulder made her jump.

"Hey! You made it!" said a voice in her ear.

"Oh hi, Tyler," Missy said casually, as Casey whipped around to look at him.

He grinned. His hair was damp from a shower and a cowlick made it curl loosely on his forehead. "Hi," she said, suppressing the urge to reach out and push that hair aside with her fingers.

"Now we'll see if the bullpen can make Doggy's dinger stand up," he said to Missy.

Casey blinked. "Is everything baseball players say obscene?"

He and Missy laughed. "I'll translate," she said, putting her hand on Casey's forearm. "Doggy, that's my husband. A 'dinger' is a home run, I guess because in the old days they rang a bell when you hit one. And to make a score 'stand up' means making sure it's enough. So if they win the game two to nothing, then two runs will not have been knocked down by the other team scoring more."

Tyler smirked. "You're as smart as your husband."

"I still think it sounds dirty," Casey said.

He shrugged. "You really don't know anything about baseball, do you?"

"Well, I know there are three outs in an inning and that Babe Ruth was the greatest player, but that's about it." She crossed her arms.

But he looked delighted. "Let's get out of here. You deserve a nice dinner out for sitting through all this."

THE HOT STREAK

Casey was about to say no. She should have said no. But she hesitated a little too long.

"I'll get us a private table at Blu. Come on, it's on *me*," he emphasized, as if she might have declined because the place was too expensive for her. Which it was.

"I'm not dressed for..."

"Did you miss the part about the private table? Besides, it's summer. You look fine."

The approving look Missy was giving her clinched it, though. "Oh, all right."

"Excellent!" He jumped like a little boy, took Casey's hand and pulled her up the aisle while she waved goodbye to Missy.

～

Simply put, dinner with Tyler at a ridiculously fancy restaurant wasn't anything like Casey expected it would be.

He'd driven them from the ballpark to the Ritz-Carlton downtown in his sports car—it was the first time she'd considered there was a connection between "sports" and sports cars—and she kept thinking if he was really going to put a move on her, they'd have champagne on ice and caviar brought to their private dining room while a white-gloved staff, silent and discreet, served the courses and swapped out the correct forks and knives.

But when they got there, the first thing that happened at the doorway to the restaurant was the *maitre d'* began to chew Tyler out. "Mr. Hammond, nice to see you as always, but what were you thinking plunking Campbell like that?"

Tyler just shrugged. "What's the score?"

The man pulled his phone out of the breast pocket of his jacket. "Three-zip."

"How'd we get the third run?"

"Go in the bar and watch it on ESPN if you want the details," was the reply. Then he looked at Casey. "Or would you like a table for two?"

Tyler glanced at Casey as well. "Up to you."

"Me?" That came out far too much like a squeak for Casey's comfort, and she told herself to calm down. "Um..."

The *maitre d'* was a broad man, but couldn't have been more than twenty-five. He addressed Tyler again. "They're about to quit serving in the main dining room, actually. But the bar's dead. Tuesday night in the summer, you know."

"Sure. I'll keep Hojo company. The bar all right with you?" he asked, one hand hovering behind Casey's shoulder blade.

Maybe this really was just a casual thing. She wasn't sure if that was a relief or a disappointment. "Sure. The bar sounds great."

Tyler and the beefy *maitre d'* exchanged hand slaps like they were teammates and Tyler steered her toward the artfully lit modern-art style bar. Down at the far end, a bartender was watching the game on a widescreen TV. There was a single businessman sitting near the door; otherwise, the place was empty.

"My man!" The bartender said as Tyler and Casey approached. He reached over the taps and they exchanged a fancy handshake. He was a wiry fellow with horn-rimmed glasses. "Here a bit early, aintcha?"

"Not really," Tyler said. "You know they would've yanked me after the seventh anyway." He slid onto a stool. "Hojo, this is Casey."

"Nice to meet you," Casey said and extended her hand for a perfectly normal handshake.

THE HOT STREAK

Tyler proceeded to rattle off what he wanted to eat, punctuated by occasional questions to Casey. Did she eat shrimp? Was she okay with fried things? Allergic to anything? Hojo went to put in the order.

"I take it you eat here a lot," Casey said.

"Yeah, you could say that. This is the hotel where our team stayed when I played for the Blue Jays, and I liked it, so when I moved into town, I kept coming back." He stood halfway on his barstool, reached behind the bar for two glasses and the beverage gun, and filled one glass with club soda for himself. "What do you like?"

Casey had her hand over her mouth. "You're allowed to do that?"

"Why not? What're they going to do, throw us out? Hojo's a friend, we're doing him a favor doing his job for him." He waved the gun impatiently.

"Oh, uh, sure. Club soda."

"You got it." He filled her glass.

When the bartender came back, Tyler scoffed. "What kind of a place is this? No ice in the drinks!"

Hojo rolled his eyes and scooped a couple of cubes into each glass. "So, you guys want cocktails, too?"

"He's the best mixmeister in the...aw, damn!" Tyler broke off as the image on the television showed a home run leaving the ballpark.

"It's cool, man, it's cool," Hojo said. "Just a solo shot. Rigney will nail it down."

"Who's Rigney?" Casey asked, sipping her club soda and watching Tyler's face, as his eyes were now glued to the screen.

"He's our stopper," Tyler said, and Casey pictured a cork,

bobbing on a pond of water. "Always pitches the ninth inning, and only when we have a lead," he clarified.

"Rig's cool," Hojo said. "When you bringing him around here again? I got balls for him to sign."

"Ah, you know him." Tyler took a sip of his club soda, then rolled the glass in his hand, picking up condensation on his fingers. "Doesn't drink. Tell him there's a Bible meeting here, though, and he'll be first in line."

They chuckled at that.

The food began arriving then, and the game ended with the Robins winning. "Nice," Tyler said, as the final score flashed up on the screen. "That saves my bacon."

"How?" Casey asked, eating another piece of delicately fried shrimp wrapped in sliced mango.

"You know, I got myself tossed from the game. If we lost, it'd be my fault for losing my head. But Javy and the guys held it together, didn't they? They can take all the credit, too. I'll probably still get fined, though." He licked his fingers.

"For fighting?"

"And for leaving early. Although I did go up to the press box and give the writers all the quotes they wanted before I came down to get you."

"You talked to the press?"

"Oh, yeah. Normally I'd wait around down in the clubhouse and after the game, they'd swarm me." He shrugged. "But I was hoping you were there."

He said it so casually, Casey could almost dismiss it. "How much are they going to fine you?"

"Dunno." He took a piece of shrimp in his fingers and popped it into his mouth. "Probably a couple thousand dollars."

THE HOT STREAK

"A couple thousand dollars?" She knew her eyes must be as wide as the TV above them. He'd basically just admitted that he'd paid a few thousand dollars just for the chance to go out with her.

"Yeah," he said. "So, isn't the food here amazing? Try this thing here." He pulled over a plate they hadn't started on yet, another appetizer that seemed to have cucumber rounds heaped with some kind of sushi. He held one between his fingers, which Casey noticed were very long and thin, his nails perfectly trimmed. "Try it."

She hadn't eaten from a man's hand since she was in college, probably. The guys she normally went out with were always trying so hard to impress her with how grown up they were—and she did the same to them. Almost thirty, not yet married, she was tired of men whose goal in life seemed to be to prove they could act like her Dad.

She took the cucumber into her mouth. It had a cool crunch, which offset how the fish seemed to just melt with tangy spices. "Damn, that's good," she said, one hand over her mouth as she was still chewing.

"I know! It's awesome. They only have it when the tuna is fresh caught." He put one into his own mouth, tipping his head back and groaning with pleasure as he chewed. It was a nice sound, Casey thought. Well, a naughty sound, really.

The conversation ranged over many topics. Whether golf was a real sport and whether Casey would need to learn to play it if she were to become a manager at her company. Pros and cons of vegetarianism. Hybrid cars.

Hojo brought more food. Tiny medallions of lamb, velvet soft and barely needing a knife to be cut, and some kind of fish filet rolled with crabmeat. Everything was delicious, and Tyler wanted to share it all, each of them eating bits from whatever plate struck their fancy. No, it wasn't anything at all like what Casey had expected going to one of the fanciest restaurants in the city would be like.

She was wiping up the sauce the lamb had come in with a piece of a whole grain roll when Tyler said, "Wow, I like you. You're a real girl."

Casey chuckled and took a bite. "What do you mean?"

"I mean, just...you know...well, maybe you don't know. I keep going out with these girls who are like, 'oh, I can't eat carbs because I'm watching my figure. And I can't eat fat because it's bad for my skin. And I can't drink because I'll bloat. And I can't have ice cream because dairy gives me bags under my eyes...'"

"What are they, supermodels?" Casey quipped.

"Well, actually, yeah," Tyler said with a shrug, reaching over the bar to snag the gun and refill his soda water. "Or sometimes not, but they act like they are. You seem like you know how to enjoy life."

"Funny," she said, realizing he was not only complimenting her, he was being plain and honest. "I was going to say the same thing about you."

"And here's the thing," he said, taking a gulp of soda, setting the glass down, and turning his bar stool so his knees faced her. "You look just as fantastic, in fact maybe twice as fantastic, as any of those Botox diet bunnies do, and it's not because you're killing yourself for some kind of fucked-up beauty ideal. It's because you're just plain beautiful."

If they had been drinking something other than soda water, Casey would have blamed his candor on alcohol. As it was, she just blushed and smiled. "Are you high?" she joked.

THE HOT STREAK

"High on life," he said, knocking back the rest of the soda, the ice clinking in the glass as he set it down with a sigh. "You've got work tomorrow, huh?"

Casey bit her lip. It was almost midnight now as it was, and attractive and thrilling and interesting as Tyler Hammond was—the image of the woman at the ballpark screaming "I love you, Tyler!" ran through her mind. "Um, yeah," she said, while kicking herself for sounding so inarticulate. Here this guy had just said one of the nicest and most honest things she thought she'd heard a man say to her in years, and all she could muster in response were monosyllables. "Look, it's not that I don't like you, but I really do have a meeting at nine thirty."

"All right," he said. "You pick the date for the next one. If you're interested, that is." He raised his eyebrow a little, as if challenging her to chicken out.

"Fine." She put down her napkin and smirked. "Make it Saturday, then. I'll have no excuses."

"Saturday it is," he said with a nod, standing up and reaching out a hand to help her from her stool. His hands were gentle and surprisingly soft on hers as he did, not at all what she expected from a jock. Her shoulder tingled where his fingers had brushed her as she stood.

He drove her home, pulling up by the fire hydrant outside her building and putting the car into park with the blinkers on as he spoke. "Okay, so, just so we're clear on things, I don't want you to think I'm one of those guys who puts a last-minute move on a girl just to see if she'll give in and invite me up. But I do want you to know that it's totally okay if you don't want a goodnight kiss, but I did consider this sort of a first date, you know, and so I'd really like one. But only if it's okay with you."

He delivered the entire speech with both hands on the steering wheel, staring at the rim, but then turned and looked at her. Casey stared at him. "You say some of the oddest things," she said.

"Yeah, that's what Mad Dog says, too. So was that a yes or a no?"

"Um..." Casey felt like she could hear her heart beating in her chest.

"My Daddy always said if a lady isn't sure, that means no." His shoulders slumped a little.

Casey snorted. "I'm not a lady," she said. She realized *she'd* feel disappointed if they didn't kiss, and that decided her. "Come here."

He leaned toward her then, and she slid her hands up his smooth cheeks. He must have shaved when he showered after leaving the game, she thought, as she pulled him forward a bit more so that she could press her lips to his. They were firm, and warm, and she breathed in that heady mixture of his cologne and the air he exhaled.

She drew back. "Saturday," she said.

"Saturday," he repeated, like it was a secret code word. He waved to her with a huge grin on his face as she backed out of the car, then, and even something about the way he drove off made her think, *Wow, he really likes me.*

CHAPTER TWO

Casey found herself reading the sports page in the company cafeteria the next day. There were large photos in color of Tyler being tossed from the game, and many articles mentioning his name. *Funny what you can learn from the paper*, she thought. The articles helpfully pointed out certain things she hadn't felt comfortable asking, like the fact that he was twenty-four years old, grew up in Kalamazoo, Michigan, and was the oldest of three brothers. The other two were baseball players, too, but neither one was as good or as famous as Tyler. She also found out that there had been exactly 42,018 people at the game the night before. Sports writing, she decided, depended on a lot of random facts to make up for the fact that the articles were mostly expressing some guy's opinion about what had happened. For the hell of it, she cut out one of the pictures of Tyler and tacked it on the bulletin board above her desk.

She combed the paper the next day for information about him but found it lacking. Mark from Accounting explained the pitching rotation to her: five different guys took turns being the starting pitcher, so Sunday's paper would probably be full of stuff about him. She wondered if Tyler would ask her to come see him pitch again.

It wasn't until Friday that it struck her that if he pitched on Sunday, that meant that although Saturday wasn't a "school night" for her, it was for him. But she got an e-mail from him late that afternoon confirming their plans, telling her to dress casually, so she decided not to say anything about it.

Friday night was an utter bust, too, as she was talked into going out with a bunch of the girls from work to a big pool hall. That in and of itself wouldn't have been so bad, except they were all younger than her, most of them met up with their boyfriends once they arrived, and Casey wasn't really that interested in playing pool. She ended up drifting away from the group into the bar, where many televisions were playing baseball games and a few other sports. At least half the screens were showing the Robins, though.

"They're losing?" she asked a forty-ish looking man at the bar while waiting for the bartender to pour her drink.

"Yeah, this'll be four in a row they dropped," he said, sounding disgusted.

"Really? I was at the game Monday and they won. It was really exciting."

He shrugged. "It's still early in the season, but I'm not getting my hopes up."

She took the drink and sipped it, wondering about that. She knew in a purely academic way that there were people who were into sports. People who followed their teams like some kind of religion or family tradition. But she hadn't realized just how ubiquitous it was. What other thing could she just walk up to a total stranger and make a random comment about? The weather?

"What do you think of Tyler Hammond?" she asked, just to see what the fellow would say.

He cracked a grin. "He's a nutball, but he's our nutball," he said. "I picked him before the season to win the Cy Young Award. That was before he lost four straight starts last month."

"Ah," she said, as if she knew what he was talking about. "He was doing well Monday until he got ejected from the game."

"Yeah," the guy said, eyes on the screen rather than on her as he talked. "Maybe he'll get on a hot streak now. That'd be nice."

He went back to watching the game, she went back to the pool table to watch politely for a short while, and then went home as early as was polite.

Tyler picked her up at six thirty the next evening.

"Did you get my e-mail?" were the first words out of his mouth as she slid into the bucket seat.

"Other than the one I replied to?" she asked, puzzled.

"Oh, right. Of course." He smacked himself on the forehead, which gave her the urge to giggle but she suppressed it. "Yeah, so, I guess you did. Dress casually, I mean."

Casey was wearing a nice-looking warm-up suit her mother had given her for Christmas—along with a three-month gym membership that Casey had used exactly four times. And she hadn't worn the warm-up suit once. It was far too nice to get all dirty on the floor in a yoga class. "Is this all right? Where are we going?"

"It's perfect," he said, leaning over to kiss her on the cheek, and then looking at oncoming traffic as he signaled to pull out.

"Just perfect. We're going to the driving range."

"Oh, you mean like golf?" She had a vague memory of the driving range being a place her dad went from time to time. "Well, you said if you're going to be a manager, you need to play golf." He weaved between a garbage truck and an SUV into the left lane. "The driving range is the place to start if you want to learn golf. Or if you just have frustrations to get out and you want to whack the hell out of that little ball."

Now she did laugh. "Oh, I have frustrations to get out. Work is driving me nuts."

"Me, too," he said.

"Oh, did the team lose again today?" she asked as they crossed the boulevard onto the river road.

He gave an exaggerated sigh, which was all the answer that was necessary. "Let's not talk about the Robins, all right?"

"All right. What do you want to talk about?"

He looked blank for a moment. "I don't want you to think I'm one of those guys who only wants to talk about himself or his job..."

She put a hand on his shoulder. "How about this? When you get boring, I'll tell you."

"You promise?"

"I promise."

"Because I really could talk about baseball and the Robins and pitching and stuff like that all day." He punched a button on the dashboard radio and the sound of a sports talk radio station played in the car. He fiddled with the dial a moment, and then said, "Could you find something else?"

"Sure." She poked at the buttons, changing it from AM to FM and searching for a station. "What kind of music do you like?"

"Anything fast," he said, passing another sports car as the traffic opened up.

As it was, they didn't talk about baseball, or Tyler, very much on the drive. And once they reached the driving range, there were things to talk about, like balls and clubs and swings.

Tyler bought a bucket of balls for ten bucks, then showed her to a kind of stall, facing a large field surrounded by netting. There were small white signs with numbers on them showing the distance. "Okay, so I'm going to say a whole lot, then demonstrate it, but what it comes down to ultimately is...you're going to whack the hell out of that little ball."

"So you've said."

"Right." He showed her how to hold the club then, his large, warm hands covering hers. He had long fingers, she noticed, as he adjusted her grip. He explained how to set her feet, how to use her hip to turn and drive the ball. Then he motioned her to step back, and he took a few practice swings, then hit the ball with a satisfying *thwack*.

He looked up in time to see it bounce to a stop just past the sign painted with the number 200.

"Is that two hundred feet?" she asked.

"God, I hope not," he said, looking a bit deflated. "I'm hoping that's two hundred yards."

Then it was Casey's turn. She took her place in front of the tee while he put a ball down, then fiddled with her hands. "Um, would you show me that grip again?"

She blushed as he did it, because she didn't really need the help; she just wanted to feel his hands again. She hoped it didn't seem glaringly obvious, though. He was warm as he reached around her. He was so much taller than she was, so he could stand behind her and grip her hands in his, enveloping her in his arms. Once her hands were in place, he stepped back again.

"All right," he said. "Let her rip."

She drew the club back, picturing all the TV commercials she'd ever seen that showed Tiger Woods hitting a ball, then swung it as hard as she could. The club made a sharp whooshing sound and she ended up with it behind her back, looking out at the grass. "Where did it go?"

He was chuckling and she looked down and saw the ball was still sitting, unperturbed, on the tee. She started to laugh, too.

"But your form looked great!" Tyler said. "Don't change anything. Except the actual hitting the ball part."

Casey took another swing. This one connected and she felt the impact all the way up her arms. And the ball flew, up and up, then down to bounce somewhere past the 100-yard sign.

"How did that feel?" Tyler asked, not even looking at where the ball went.

"Pretty good."

"Hit another one!" He gave her a bright grin as he put down another ball. "Go on!"

She did. After about ten swings, they switched places and he hit a dozen balls out into the field. Other people were hitting, too, unseen from their vantage point in the stall, and to Casey it looked like the balls were following each other, like frogs jumping into a pond.

She could hardly believe it when the bucket was empty. "That was really a hundred?"

"Well, fifty or so each, yeah," Tyler said, one hand on his shoulder as he windmilled his arm around. "You want to hit some more? You're going to be sore tomorrow."

She couldn't let a straight line like that go by. She put a hand on his cheek and batted her eyelashes. "Oh, am I?"

"Um..." Tyler abandoned the attempt to phrase a witty comeback and instead slid his hands around her waist and put his forehead against hers. "Yeah," he finally said, voice a bit gravelly. "Yeah, I sure hope so."

She tipped her face up for a quick kiss, then glanced around quickly. He did the same, like two teenagers afraid to get caught. "What's next?" she asked.

"Well, are you hungry? We could go and get..."

She found herself pulling him close by his belt loops. "I am hungry."

"Oh..."

It seemed she had made herself clear. They returned the bucket and were soon in the car again, Casey running a hand up his thigh as he backed out of the parking space. Truth was, she'd been wondering what sex would be like with Tyler all week. Ever since that chaste goodnight kiss.

There were plenty of reasons, or so advice columnists might tell her, she suspected, why she should wait. *String him along a little more. He'll respect you more. Prove you're not a fan. Make sure he's serious about you and not just getting laid.* And on and on.

But she didn't want to wait. She was tired of men who respected her and who were nice and kind and loving and who seemed really hopeful and optimistic about "building something together," but whom she tended to drop after the third or fourth date because they were crummy in bed. Or maybe they were okay, but they didn't really turn her on. Dating had become a sort of chore, like apartment hunting or car maintenance.

THE HOT STREAK

But Tyler was not a chore date. He wasn't a friend of a friend, a blind date, or from an online matchmaker. He was something totally out of the blue.

He drove them to his apartment, a high-rise building not far from the Ritz with an underground parking garage, which was handy, she thought, because it beat circling around her neighborhood looking for a place to put the car. They rode up in a private elevator straight from the garage that Tyler had to put his key in to allow it to reach his floor.

Then they were inside a quiet, high-ceilinged modern apartment that didn't really look very lived in. He pulled her into the kitchen. "Something to drink?" He opened the fridge. "Rum and Coke? I know I have both of those. Or sparkling water?"

She held in a goofy grin. "Sparkling water would be great."

He searched around a bit for the glasses. "I only moved in here last month. And the team's been on the road more than half of that. So I'm still figuring out where everything is. A moving company did all the unpacking. And you know, I barely eat here."

He was sweet, she decided. Sweetly nervous, but not in a wimpy way. He brought her the glass of fizzy water and lingered next to her, leaning against the counter, close enough that she could feel the warmth emanating from his skin. She sipped and looked up at him, and he slid an arm around her waist. Not in a hurry, drinking his water. Casey could hear them both breathing, hear the slight tinkling sound of the fizz in the glasses. He wasn't like one of the fake macho guys who put on a Casanova act—and he wasn't afraid either.

"I think I've had enough water," she said, setting her glass down on the granite countertop and leaning into him.

She heard his glass land on the counter as well, then he cradled her face in his hands and pulled her into a kiss. Her tongue tingled as if she were still drinking when it softly touched his.

"Bedroom?" she whispered softly against his lips.

"Yeah, I think I can find that," he answered.

Everything in the bedroom was gray. Slate gray, steel gray, dove gray, with wide flat windows covering one wall and overlooking the park. It looked like a spread out of a home design catalog.

The one colorful thing was a bright red pillow in the shape of a bird, sitting in a chair off to one side. Casey went and picked it up. It was covered with signatures in black magic marker and messages like, "Good Luck Tyler" and "Go Hammer."

"Oh, uh," he explained, "my mom's an elementary school teacher. Every season she sends me something from all the kids in her class. For luck. It doesn't matter where I'm pitching, she turns them all into fans of whatever team it is." He put his arms around her from behind. "I haven't had a losing season yet, so she just keeps doing it."

She leaned back into him, pleased by the warm feeling of his lips against her temple. "Are you superstitious about it?"

"Yeah, I guess." He worked his way down to her neck, pausing between kisses to speak. "All ballplayers are. You figure, don't mess with what works."

Then his mouth was too busy suckling at the join of her neck and shoulder to say any more, and her own mouth was letting out soft cries of encouragement. Oh damn, that felt good.

He pulled her down with him onto the bed, him sitting with her in his lap. She was kicking off her shoes then, while his hands reached around her to unzip the jacket of her warm-up suit. When it was open, he slipped his hands under the edge of her shirt, thumb and forefinger circling her waist and caressing back and forth. She tilted her head so she could kiss him, sloppy but heated, and his fingertips slipped up her ribcage to the edge of her breasts, just cupping gently at the swell of flesh.

"No bra?" he breathed into her ear.

"Never needed one," she answered.

"Excellent." He let his hands slide further up, until she gasped as his fingers stroked lightly across her nipples. She arched in his lap, wanting more, and her nipples were not the only thing becoming erect.

He slipped the jacket off her, then eased her T-shirt over her head, leaving her half-naked in his lap. His hands returned to her breasts, circling her nipples and tweaking them gently between his finger and thumb, then rolling the hardened points in the center of his palms. She gasped in pleasure and banked desire. Plenty of guys liked to play with her breasts, but most of them liked to stare at them. Tyler was giving them plenty of attention, the soft moans of his own proving that he was enjoying it as much as she did, but it felt different. Good. It felt good. What it *didn't* feel like was that he had won a prize to look at her tits and that he was now memorizing what they looked like for his own personal memory-porn bank.

"Shift up a little," he rasped, hooking his thumbs in the waistband of her sweatpants, and she did as he slid them halfway down her thighs easily.

It wasn't until his hand brushed over her mound that she realized he'd slid her panties down as well.

"All right?" he asked, nuzzling her hair.

"Yeah," she answered. She would have spread her legs to encourage him, but her own pants trapped her knees together. She felt him petting her fur, three fingers stroking gently over and over, until the middle one started to go further, applying a bit more pressure than the other two. It slipped between her lips, brushing over her clit, and she gasped, clutching at him behind her. He rocked his hand back and forth, murmuring appreciatively about how wet she was.

She felt like her clit was swollen, like the sopping wetness his touches had brought out had waterlogged it and made it grow to twice its size. Twice as sensitive, too. Now his finger was moving in slow circles, and she moaned, squirming a bit in his lap.

"How many times do you like to come?" he asked.

"What?" she said, not sure she'd heard him correctly through her haze of lust.

"Are you one-and-done, or do you like to have more?"

She found herself chuckling. "One-and-done? Is that a...a phrase?"

He nuzzled in her ear as he spoke, as he stroked her. "Well, it is, but it usually refers to guys who are stingy with giving, if you know what I mean. I'm not one of those. If you want to come, just say 'Tyler, make me come,' or something like that."

"Is that fair, really?" she asked, lifting her hands behind her head to run her fingers through his hair. "I mean, guys can only have one. I don't want to be...selfish."

He laughed. "I can tell already you're not some Do-Me-Queen. So tell me. You want me to make you come now, here like this, or just...tease you some more?"

No one had ever asked Casey a question like that in bed before, one that was a real question and a turn-on all at once.

THE HOT STREAK

She was tempted to say *yes, do it, make me come...* but it was all a tease for what she really wanted, wasn't it? "I want to put my arms around you," she said. "I want to kiss you." She found herself hesitating, though.

"Mmm, and?" he asked, hearing that she was not done.

"And I want to come while you're inside me." There, it was said. She knew her cheeks were burning. She wasn't one for talking dirty. And that was the thing: nothing Tyler had said was particularly raunchy or felt like it was supposed to be. He really wanted to know.

And she really wanted to answer. And she had. He stroked her a bit longer and then said, "There's no rush. But I'm game."

He stood her up with careful hands on her hips, then slid her pants the rest of the way down so she could step out. He paused to hug her, and Casey shivered delightedly at her naked skin against his clothing. It was a thrilling feeling. But it might be even more thrilling to feel skin against skin. "You're over-dressed," she said, half in a whisper.

He chuckled. "Getting there."

He sat back down on the bed and leaned over to untie his shoes. Casey clambered behind him and stroked her fingers through his hair while he shucked his jeans. She helped him pull his polo shirt off, and they crawled together toward the center of what seemed like an enormous bed.

She got her first good look at him naked when she turned around to see him settling on his side next to her. Outside the sun was setting over the park, and his skin seemed to glow in the fading light, in the grayness of the room. She put a tentative hand on his hip, not feeling quite bold enough to just reach out and grab him.

"Can I...can I put the condom on you?" she asked, breathless and eager.

"I would love it if you would," he said, rolling away from her briefly to pull something out of the drawer in the bedside table, then rolling back with the little packet in his fingers.

"Lie back, then," she said, biting her lip as she smiled.

"Yes, ma'am." He smirked, then dropped his mouth open in a silent "ah" as she stroked him once, twice, before pushing the cool rubber against the head. He felt like steel in her hands, his pulse seeming to beat through her fingertips, as she covered him. His voice was breathless now. "Do you want to be on top?"

She shook her head, giving him a joking punch on the arm. "Nah. It's too much work."

He laughed, flipping her over with a warm hand on her hip. Those hands, those long fingers. She sighed, parting her legs.

He settled himself between her knees, nuzzling softly at her breasts and kissing her nipples, then shifting himself toward the head of the bed, until she could feel the length of him rubbing her clit as he rutted against her. She found her hands tugging on his buttocks, trying to encourage him to penetrate her, not just rub back and forth on her

He nodded as if he heard the unspoken plea, shifting down again, his angle changing, and then..."Ohhh."

He slid in easily. When was the last time she was this wet? He rocked a bit, side to side, working his way in deeper, then resting a moment before pulling all the way out, slipping his thumb over her clit a few times, and pushing into her again.

The next thing she knew, he was going at it steadily, his rhythm slow but not stopping, supporting his weight on his left arm while his right thumb slipped down over her clit on every stroke. God, he felt good. Inside her, and touching her, and she felt it wouldn't be long before she came, especially as close as he'd brought her earlier.

"Tyler..." she said, as her arousal leaped up another notch. "Gonna come..."

"I know, darling, I know. Go right ahead."

And there she was, at the top, like a sudden ray of sunlight seen over the crest of a hill, the moment blinding and beautiful as she fell down the other side with a cry. He moved in and out of her, all through the spasms of her orgasm, and it felt better and better, as if he were massaging her inside. She clutched him suddenly, feeling like a second orgasm might follow quickly on the heels of the first.

"Harder?" he asked, propping himself back a little to look at her face.

She nodded, and as he picked up the pace there it was again. "Oh, God..." She wrapped her legs around him, pulling him deeper, as the sensation blossomed from her middle, tingling and sending sparks all the way to the tips of her toes.

When she opened her eyes, he was looking at her face, rapt. "You're so..."

"You, now," she urged, cutting off whatever he had been about to say. "You, now, Tyler." God, he'd reduced her to short words, sentence fragments.

But he understood. "Yes, ma'am. Hold on." He sped up once again, stomach muscles clenching. She ran her hands all over him, feeling how firm his muscles were. Perhaps there were advantages to dating a professional athlete that should have been obvious to her, but which she hadn't really grasped until now, when she could see his washboard abs as he snapped his hips forward, feel the muscles in his arms.

He grunted, said, "Casey," then grunted again, a longer one, cock twitching inside her, and then slowed suddenly. "Oh, Casey." He kissed her then, a warm and tender meeting of lips, as if he hadn't just been going at it like a porn star. "Wow."

"Wow," she agreed. She could feel him gradually softening until he could no longer keep up the motion and slipped free. He rolled onto his side and kept an arm around her.

"Wow," he said again.

"Wow," she answered, starting to giggle a little.

She felt him smile as he kissed her neck. "I'd say 'wow' again, except I'm too wiped out."

"Not too wiped out to pitch tomorrow, though?" she asked, finally giving voice to the nagging thought she'd been suppressing all evening.

He chuckled. "Figured that out, did you? No worries. I'll be fine. It's a national game. Doesn't start until the evening. I don't need to be there until about three in the afternoon. Which means we can sleep until at least noon. And it's"—he turned over to look at the clock—"not even ten at night. Although we haven't had dinner yet."

It sounded like he was asking her to stay the night. She hadn't brought any clothes or anything with her, but she said, "Sleeping 'til noon sounds nice. So does dinner. But right now I just want to lie here."

"Let's get under the covers, then." He shifted and they slid under cool sheets toward one side of the bed.

She ran her hands over his skin now, sweat cooling and making his skin surprisingly silky. "What's this?" she asked, running her fingertips over the ridge of a scar at his elbow.

"Oh, that's from my Tommy John surgery."

"Who?"

THE HOT STREAK

"Wow, you really don't know anything about baseball, do you?"

She shook her head. "Was Tommy John...oh no, wait, I was going to ask you about Cy Young. I was talking to a guy yesterday who said he hoped you'd win the Cy Young Award."

He laughed. "One at a time. Tommy John was a pitcher in the '70s who had surgery to repair his pitching elbow, and now everyone who has that surgery names it after him. And lots and lots of pitchers have it. Cy Young, on the other hand, was a great pitcher in like 1910. So they give the best pitcher of the year what they call the Cy Young Award."

Casey nodded, running her fingers over the scar again. "Sounds like baseball likes to commemorate players by naming things after them. Though it sounds better to have an award named after you instead of a surgical procedure."

Tyler shrugged. "I guess I'd settle for being remembered, however it was going to happen. Knowing me, they'll name a new rule after me that limits the number of times per season a pitcher can be ejected, or something like that."

"Hm. Don't get ejected tomorrow."

"Why?"

"Because I want to see you pitch. And you can't win the Cy Young Award if you get thrown out all the time."

"True."

They lay in comfortable silence after that, and Casey felt herself drifting to sleep. She wondered if this sort of evening with Tyler was going to become a regular thing. She hoped it would.

Little did she know it was about to become more regular than she could have imagined

.

CHAPTER THREE

Casey and Tyler slept late, then grabbed brunch at a restaurant just off the Common. It was sunny, but the wind seemed a bit chilly.

"Can you believe it's the first week of June?" Tyler complained and asked for a table inside instead of on the patio. "And it was so warm the other night when I pitched. It's so much easier when it's warm out. The ball feels better. It flies farther, too, in hot air."

"It does?" It never occurred to her that the weather was such a factor, other than that they didn't play if it rained too hard. And some sports didn't even bother with that. She settled into her chair, wondering if it the game tonight was going to be chilly, too. "Hey, so why is it that baseball gets called off if it rains, but football they play in the rain, snow, bitter cold...?"

Tyler made a disgusted noise. "Because they're crazy, that's why. Make fifty thousand people sit through a snowstorm where they can't even see the game? But really, it's that baseball is too dangerous if the field is too wet or if you can't see well. You get hit in the helmet with a football, you won't even feel it, but take a fastball in the face? Guys have died from it. Well, one guy, back in the day, and that was enough. They don't take chances. Besides, we play 162 regular-season games a year. Football plays only sixteen. They can't afford to skip one, and they can't play doubleheaders like we can, either."

She chuckled. This was possibly the most macho she'd seen Tyler so far, defending the toughness of his sport in the face of the comparison to football. "All right, all right. I wasn't implying baseball is a pansy sport or anything."

"Damn straight," he said, then ordered enough food for a family of four from the perky young waitress who had appeared with her pen at the ready.

"That all for you?" Casey asked. "Or is that for both of us?"

"I was thinking just for me, but we can share if you want...?"

She handed the menu to the waitress. "Add one blueberry nut waffle to the order and I'm good. Oh, and a cup of tea."

They sat in silence for a while, watching other patrons rushing around. Some were families in their Sunday best, coming from the big churches on the other side of the park, plus couples young and old, and a group of college students taking up one corner. The sound of the espresso machine hissed over it all.

"So, you're coming to the game tonight, right?"

Casey looked at him. He was trying to sound casual, but there was a note mixed in there that sounded just a little like a puppy's whine.

"Sure, of course," she said. "Can you fix it so Missy and I sit together again? She's awesome."

"Done!" Tyler clapped his hands and a huge grin spread

across his face. "And yeah, she is pretty cool, huh? Mad Dog would be lost without her. They got hitched when he was still in the minor leagues. Real young. But they've made it work, they've made it last. They're coming up on ten years or something soon."

"Ten...?"

"Yeah, they got married right after he got drafted in college, before he went to his first minor league assignment. He was like, maybe, twenty? She stayed and finished school and then moved out to be with him, and he's turning thirty this year, so yeah, ten years." He was staring at the water glass in front of him. "Sounds like a lot, doesn't it?"

"It does. I'm lucky if a relationship lasts ten months."

That made him crack a grin. "Yeah, me too. So you want to take bets on how long we'll last?"

She snorted. "That's a losing bet no matter what, then. No way."

"Okay. Let's just see what happens, eh?"

"Sounds like a plan." She looked up as the waitress dropped off her tea, coffee for Tyler, and a basket of warm muffins. That was possibly one of the shortest, easiest "relationship discussions" she'd ever had. Of course, it helped that they agreed. How novel.

She decided to go home and get warmer clothes before heading to the ballpark that night, so after they were done eating, they went their separate ways.

Her apartment seemed especially quiet that afternoon and, her usual Sunday things like the crossword puzzle not holding her interest, she set about tidying up a bit,. She ended up booting up her laptop and checking her e-mail, then looking at the weather.

The Hot Streak

She could hear her cell phone ringing and dug it hurriedly out of her jacket pocket, thinking it would be Tyler. But she didn't recognize the number. It was showing a Chicago area code. "Hello?"

"Casey? It's Kim! How are you?"

"I'm good. What are you doing in Chicago?"

"I'm calling to give you my new number and stuff. I just moved here. It's awesome. You'll never guess who I'm working for here."

Casey sat back down at her desk and got ready to write Kim's new information down on a pad. "Do I have to guess?"

"Come on, guess. It's an internationally known corporation with headquarters in Chicago."

"Jeez. Um..." Casey racked her brain. Kim was a writer and editor. She had been working for an agriculture trade magazine in the Napa Valley last she'd heard, and had been at a string of local newspapers before that, in Delaware, Illinois, Wisconsin. Who had their headquarters in Chicago? "Sears?"

"Nope. Think media."

"Um. WGN, the cable TV station?"

She could hear Kim's laugh, very tinny through the phone. "No."

"You better just tell me. I don't know squat about Chicago."

"It's *Playboy*."

"*Playboy Magazine*?"

"The *Playboy* media empire. Neat, huh? The pay is fantastic and I have an unbelievable apartment overlooking the lake, and when are you coming to visit?"

"Whoa, Kim, slow down."

"They give you paid vacation there and stuff, right? You've

been there long enough to qualify? Come for a long weekend. We'll do the town. I can get us into all the best places. This job rocks."

Casey couldn't help but giggle a little at Kim's enthusiasm. "I'll check my calendar when I get to work tomorrow. Drop me an e-mail to remind me, okay?"

"Okay. And you can quit thinking what you're thinking right now, by the way."

"Huh? What's that?" Casey said innocently.

"If you're thinking, isn't it gross I'm working for a porno place, and aren't I getting like sexually harassed at work every day..."

"I'm not thinking anything like that. Well, okay, I'm curious how you handle naked bunnies walking around."

Kim made a disgusted noise. "That's so not what it's about. You probably have to handle more disgusting stuff at any major ad agency than I ever will here. It's not like there are orgies in the hallways. Honestly, it's so tame and corporate, I'm almost disappointed. And *Playboy* was never really porno anyway, it's so softcore. The lad mags like *Maxim* are much worse."

"Okay, I believe you. And it beats writing about rutabagas or whatever it was you were doing before."

"No kidding. So what about you, Case? How's everything going? You getting to do more design work yet?"

Casey looked out the window and twirled her pen. "No, no designing to speak of, but...you know, the job is getting really tiresome, but I can't really complain. They keep trying to get me one more rung up into management and I keep resisting. I don't really want more responsibility, you know? I like feeling like any day I could just quit this job and walk away for another one if a better one came along."

"Is that really true, though?"

"Yeah. They'd replace me pretty quick." She chewed the end of the pen, trying to decide if she was going to tell Kim about Tyler. Maybe she should tell her a little, anyway. "So I met a guy."

"Oh? One that might make it past the blind date?"

Casey laughed. "Just had the second date last night, and I'm seeing him again tonight, sort of." She'd be watching him pitch, but the team was leaving directly after the game for a road trip, so she wouldn't have dinner with him again tonight. "And, speaking of long weekends, he's convinced me to meet him in New York this coming weekend. I'm taking Thursday and Friday off."

Kim made a scandalized noise. "So you *can* be convinced to take some time off."

"Yeah, well, they actually told me if I don't start taking some of my vacation days, I'm going to lose them. So I might as well."

"So? Are you going to tell me about him?"

"I'm trying to think of what to say."

"Uh oh."

"What do you mean, 'uh oh?'"

"That means it's really serious," Kim said. "Usually you have a little checklist of his good points to read to me like you're trying to prove when a guy is a good choice, when he really isn't."

"I do?"

"Yeah. You usually rattle off where they went to school, how much they make, dick size..."

"I have never told you a guy's dick size!"

Kim clucked her tongue. "Just an expression. If they're good in bed or not, which, yeah, you're right, you never mention, so they must all suck."

"Well, for your information, he's tall and handsome, very athletic, and really, really good in bed. And I don't actually know where he went to school or how much he makes."

"Wow. You must really like him, then."

"I have no idea where it's going. It might just be a fling, but you know what? If it is a fling, I plan to enjoy every minute of it."

"Awesome. What's his name, how'd you meet him?"

"Tyler. I met him through work on a photo shoot, but he's not a corporate type. We kind of met by chance, I guess, and just hit it off. We just think alike somehow. And he's really fun."

"He must be, if he's already taking you to New York for the weekend. That's so awesome. I'm so psyched for you, Case. When you come out to visit, you can tell me all about him. Now, I gotta run. My mom's flight lands in like an hour and the traffic here is hellacious. And you know how she'll bitch for the entire week she's here if I'm five minutes late."

"True. Take care of yourself, Kim, I'll e-mail you." Casey hung up and slipped the phone into her pocket. She and Kim had been friends since college, and they'd gotten to know each other because of a common boyfriend. Mark had been seeing them both, just not telling each other about it, and when they confronted him with it, he'd claimed he'd never promised either of them exclusivity. Somehow he hadn't seen the fact that he'd felt the need to sneak around as a form of dishonesty. Both women had been about on the verge of kicking him to the curb anyway at that point. They become fast friends after that.

THE HOT STREAK

Casey wondered when she should think about telling her family. Her little brother Nick in particular would probably be excited that she knew a professional ballplayer, though she wasn't sure he followed the sport as avidly as he had when he'd been a kid. Since he'd graduated college, she hadn't seen him that often; only at Christmas and such.

Well, it was still early. Two dates wasn't a relationship yet. Maybe when the team went to play in Philadelphia, she'd try to meet up with them. They did go to Philly, didn't they? She'd have to check the schedule. They probably went to Chicago, too, so a trip to visit Kim was looking more and more possible, the more she thought about it.

∾

By the time she got to the ballpark that night, the cold snap had really settled in. She picked up her ticket and found her way to the section easily this time. As before, she was early, and there weren't many people in that section yet, so she decided to walk around the stadium a little and see what there was to see.

She came to a little carnival at the end of one concourse, where they had stalls set up with games for kids to play. You could throw a ball and find out how fast you could throw with the radar gun, play "strike out"—knock down three bottles on three tries and win a prize—and various others. She stopped by a completely fenced-in area where kids put on a batting helmet and took a bat and faced a giant video screen. On the screen it showed a pitcher going into his windup—*Oh! That's Tyler!*—and then the ball came flying out of a little hole in the screen. The kid standing there swung at it and spun all the way around in a circle, while Casey jumped at the sound of the ball smacking into the padding right in front of her.

"Great swing!" said a pre-recorded version of Tyler's voice. "I bet you catch up to the next one."

Casey moved on. She was surprised to find a sushi bar on the concourse behind the outfield; then again, she had read a newspaper story, when she'd been looking for more information about Tyler, about how the team had a new Japanese player. Was the sushi bar to cater to his international fans? Or was the ballpark just such a hip place to be these days? She didn't know.

A little further down, she came to a stand that smelled too good to pass up. Fried chicken. She got herself a couple of pieces and a side of mashed potatoes with gravy, and chewed on the drumstick as she walked around. Soon she had walked all the way around the whole place and was back where she had started.

Missy was there in a hooded parka with her hands in mittens. "Hey, Casey, I was hoping you'd be here today."

"You were? I mean...oh, right, because Tyler pitches today."

"Yep. Every five days, sometimes six if there's a day off, but sometimes even so, and they'll skip one of the other guys instead." Missy rubbed her mittens, which were made of some fairly bright pink yarn, together. "Get used to it."

Casey settled into her seat and opened her container of mashed potatoes, stirring it with a plastic spoon to mix the gravy in. "Yeah, I guess I will. Seems..." Was she really saying this to someone she just met? "Seems like it's working out so far."

"Good!" Missy seemed like she was on the verge of saying

something, but then sat back and stuffed her mittens into her parka pockets.

"Are you really that cold?"

"I'm always cold," Missy said. "I'm from Florida. It should be against the law to play when it's this cold. At least in Toronto when it was cold, they closed the roof."

"It's like fifty degrees, though."

"Right now it is. By the fifth inning it'll be in the forties, though, and when you just sit here on your butt for a couple of hours...brrrrr. And I guarantee the concession stands are going to run out of coffee and hot chocolate."

Casey thought that was a curious thing to know. "How do you figure that?"

"The team leaves on a road trip tonight, so the concession stands are not stocking up on a lot of things. Plus it wasn't supposed to get cold like this, so they probably didn't have a lot of stuff to begin with. I'm betting by the fourth inning, there'll be not a drop to be had. If we get desperate, though, I know where we can go."

"Where?"

Missy smiled. "Let's see how it goes. Can't tell you all my secrets at once, can I? Oh, look, there go the menfolk now." She pointed to the field where Tyler, Mad Dog, and a coach had just emerged from the dugout and were walking across the grass toward the outfield again. "Such a show off," Missy went on. "They could totally go around to the bullpen through the tunnels, but Tyler wants the adoration." People around them were starting to cheer as they noticed the trio walking.

"Is that why they are walking so slowly?" Casey asked.

"Yep. And yeah, okay, they're going to play catch in the outfield first, but not all the pitchers do that."

Casey remembered the kid who got booed the previous game. "It would be pretty demoralizing to walk out there and have nobody notice you."

"Yeah, or get booed. Gooty got to the point last year where not only would he not walk across the field, he would sneak along the bullpen wall to go to the restroom so the crowd in the bleachers wouldn't boo him."

"Gooty?"

"Gutierrez, sorry. You haven't met him yet. He's on the DL."

Casey looked puzzled. "The down low?"

"The disabled list." Missy chuckled. "You really don't know anything, do you?"

"I knew what the bullpen was when you mentioned it," Casey said, although she had forgotten the name until Missy had brought it up. "But yeah, I don't know a lot about sports in general. I did stuff like figure skating and gymnastics as a kid. You know," she joked, "girly sports that people only care about during the Olympics."

Missy laughed at that. "It was ballet and jazz dance and a little bout of cheerleading for me," she said with a shrug. "Cheering is so much cooler now. Have you seen it on TV? There's tons of co-ed cheering squads, first of all, and they do all kinds of acrobatic stuff. All I did was wave some pompons around and look cute. I quit when I figured out I didn't really get along with any of the other cheerleaders, though. Frickin' shallow, catty bitches."

Casey followed Missy's eyes as she said this last, where they came to rest on a pair of women sitting several rows in front of them, both in fur coats. They were both aggressively blond. She lowered her voice. "Should I know who they are?"

"McDowell's wife, Shayna, and Riggs's wife, Michaela. They think they're the queen bees around here. Just ignore them if you can." Missy pursed her lips.

But ignoring them became difficult when the two women, as if they knew by some sixth sense they were being talked about, suddenly stood and came up the aisle.

"Oh, Missy, so glad you're here," one of them said. "Are you giving us a recipe for the cookbook? We'll need everyone for the fundraiser, too, you know. I didn't get e-mail back from you, but you know, computers, maybe it went wrong...?"

Missy's smile was a bit crooked. "Oh, yeah, must have been. Has anyone sent in a lasagna recipe yet? I could do lasagna."

The woman looked at her counterpart. "Well, Shayna here already put in a lasagna recipe."

"Oh, Missy, that's fine," said the other woman, with a dismissive flip of her hand. "I'll come up with something else, or you know, there could be two recipes in there. Could you do a low-fat or low-carb one, maybe?"

"Er, well, if you took out the pasta and the cheese," Missy said, "but that'd leave a pan of baked sauce, you know."

Shayna narrowed her eyes. Michaela patted her on the arm. "Well, send us what you can, all right? What about a nice salad? You think about it and send it along, okay?" And the two women shuffled back down to their seats.

"Wow," Casey said.

"Yeah. This is their way of telling me they want me to go on the South Beach Diet or something." She frowned in the general direction of the two women. "Subtle, aren't they? Oh, and of course I can't do lasagna, because Shayna has dibs on it, so even if she says it's okay, if I send in a lasagna recipe, she'll resent me forever."

"Looks like she already does."

"Yeah, well, funny how they don't seem to appreciate my sense of humor." Missy shrugged. "Sorry I didn't introduce you, by the way, but really, you're better off with them not paying attention to you, the miserable cows. Low fat, low carb! They're the ones who are always on diets. Why doesn't one of *them* submit a salad? Who the hell uses a cookbook to make salad anyway? God, they chap my ass."

The salty language started Casey laughing though, and then Missy was laughing, too, hiding her mouth behind her bright pink mitten.

The game started not long after that, and Casey found herself getting excited as Tyler took the mound to throw his warm-up pitches. The crowd was quite large by then, even for a cold night, and the buzz was building. He looked so tall from there, not only because he was standing on the dirt mound, but the uniform pants made his legs appear long and slender. He was wearing long sleeves under his uniform top, too, like long underwear.

The PA announcer introduced the first batter as named Franco, and a Dodgers player strode out of their dugout and took his place at the plate. Casey had a better appreciation of the glare that Tyler was giving the guy, now that she knew how odd it looked on his face. "I guess that's what they mean by 'game face,'" she said to Missy.

"Yeah. He's..." But Missy broke off as Tyler kicked and threw his first pitch right over the batter's head to the fence protecting the crowd directly behind the plate. "Oh, Jesus."

"Does he do that often? Is he hurt?"

"I don't..." Missy fell silent as she watched her husband call time and then go out to the mound as if trying to calm his pitcher down. "I don't believe this nervous act, but the rookie in the batter's box sure looks convinced." The guy practically tiptoed back into place.

The next pitch also went really wide. This time Mad Dog didn't go out to the mound, just shouted something from behind the plate, got a new ball from the umpire and tossed it to Tyler.

"They're toying with him," Missy said. "I think."

The next three pitches were strikes, "right down the middle," Missy said with glee, and the umpire did a kind of dance move that was apparently his signal to the batter to go and sit down. Now she could see Tyler holding his glove over his face, but his shoulders were shaking like he was laughing.

Missy clucked her tongue. "They made a fool of that kid Franco on national television. Sheesh. Tyler better send him a bottle of champagne and a card that says 'welcome to the big leagues.' I feel sorry for him. Well, a little. Kid'll probably hear it from all his teammates, then hit a home run next time up. Don't be surprised if their pitcher doesn't drill our shortstop in the ribs to get back at him."

It took Casey a while to realize she meant the pitcher might intentionally hit one of the Robins with the ball. The rest of the inning went well, both men hitting the ball softly to the fielders standing behind Tyler.

The next few innings went by a bit more slowly, though, as Tyler seemed to not be able to get three men in a row out; walking some, giving up some hits. He still didn't give up any runs, but it seemed like a near escape each time. The Robins got two runs on a home run in the fourth, though, and after Tyler worked his way out of a jam in the top of the fifth, Missy declared she was freezing and it was time to go in search of a hot drink.

As predicted, the concession stands were out of coffee and hot chocolate. "Come on, let's go upstairs."

"Upstairs?"

"Have you seen the luxury suite level yet? It's nice, and it's warm up there. The suites are heated and there's a big restaurant up there with a bar. They won't care if we hang out for a little while."

"We don't need special passes to be up there or something?"

"Not to ride the elevator. And they've never stopped me from sitting at the bar, either. Although the bar doesn't have coffee. Well, come on."

Casey followed her to the elevator, operated by an usher in a bright red windbreaker. They got out on the level with the luxury suites, but to Casey's surprise, Missy didn't lead her to the right following sign that read "Suites." They went left, following the sign that said "Media."

"Are you sure we're allowed to go here?" Casey said, feeling rather like they were sneaking into the backstage area at a concert.

"The writers *always* have coffee," Missy said, ignoring the question. "Even when it's ninety degrees out." She pulled open the door marked "Press Box: Media Only" and brought them face to face with a huge black man in a security guard's uniform.

"Travis!" Missy cried.

THE HOT STREAK

"Mis-sy Madison!" he answered and let her hug him, though she only came up to his chest. "How are you, girl?"

"I *love* this man," Missy said to Casey. "Don't tell Mad Dog. Trav, I'm great, but freezing my tail off. This is my friend Casey, by the way. We came searching for coffee."

"They've got a pot running in the dining room," Travis said, bowing and extending his hand as if opening an invisible door for them. "And I can smell the popcorn machine running, too."

"Ooh, so can I," Missy said as she hurried past.

"Er, thanks." Casey gave a little wave to Travis as she went by, then followed her friend into what looked like a small cafeteria. Off to one side, there were self-serve drink machines, and a set-up of glass coffeepots like Casey had seen in diners, with one pot of decaf among three caf. Next to that was a soft-serve ice cream machine, and in the corner what looked like an old-style popcorn maker on a cart, a holder on the cart's side full of paper bags. If the number of kernels scattered around on the floor was any indication, popcorn was a popular snack with the writers. "I guess they figure if they feed them, they'll be less cranky and write nicer stories?"

Missy shrugged. "I think they pay to eat dinner in here, some token amount like ten bucks or something, but yeah, seems like the snacks are free." She held a coffee cup in her hands and closed her eyes as she inhaled the steam. "What about you? Some coffee?"

"Ah, no, if I drink coffee this late, I won't get to sleep for ages. I have to be at the office at nine for a meeting."

"Ugh, poor you," Missy said, ending her communion with the steam and finally taking a sip. "I'm used to him not getting home until midnight and we'll be up until two or three a.m. sometimes after that. He doesn't have to be at the ballpark until two or three in the afternoon, so we tend to sleep from like three in the morning until eleven. It sucks when they have a day game on a Saturday or something. Well, for him. *I* sleep in."

"You don't have a job?"

"Not really. I do some volunteering kind of stuff, but it's mostly just to keep me busy when he's not around. He's making more than ten million dollars in base salary this year, so whatever paltry amount I could add to that seems kind of pointless, you know? I figure we're going to have kids soon anyway, so that'll keep me plenty busy."

They sat at a table. Across the room, a widescreen TV showed the game continuing, but Casey wasn't really paying attention to it. "Tyler was saying you guys have been married like ten years?"

"Yeah. And most of the players who marry young, they start having kids right away. But then they play, what, fifteen, twenty years including their time in the minors, if they're lucky? And just when Dad retires from baseball and is ready to spend some time with the kids, the kids are all grown up and moving out and stuff. Well, maybe they do it that way on purpose, but we didn't want it to be that way. I didn't want my kids to mostly know their father as a plaque on the wall. So we figure we'll start soon, maybe have two or three, and they'll be between four and seven or so around the time he gets ready to quit."

Casey just stared at her.

"What?"

"That's so...organized." She stared at Missy's coffee cup. "It never really occurred to me that you could plan it like that.

The Hot Streak

I always figured people just kind of...met each other, dated for a while, then got married, then had kids kind of...organically. Well, that's what I always thought would happen for me, anyway. I don't seem to get past stage one very often, though."

Missy shrugged. "I've been blessed. We were love at first sight. I never thought I was going to grow up to be a baseball wife. But as long as we have each other, you know what? I'm good with all the rest of it. Even putting up with the queen bees and everyone calling my husband Mad Dog. Hell, even I call him that now."

"It's cute," Casey said. "Although I kind of get the feeling he's a much more level-headed guy than the nickname implies. Is it like when they call a really skinny guy Fatso?"

"Yeah, I guess it is." Missy looked up suddenly. "Uh oh."

"What?" Casey looked at the TV screen. The shot was mostly of the dark sky. Then Casey realized the camera was following the trajectory of a tiny white baseball as it flew off into the night. "Oh, shit, did Tyler give them that one?"

"Looks like." Missy went over to turn up the sound but before she even got there the score updated on the screen. "Oh, jeez, that was a three-run shot. Now they're losing."

"What, no..." But there it was: Giants 3, Robins 2. "Wow, Tyler looks really pissed off." They were showing him stomping around on the mound, picking up what looked like a stuffed white sweat sock on the ground and throwing it back down, and mouthing all kinds of obscenities to himself. Then Mad Dog was there in the picture too, earnest and focused, patting him on the back and giving him some kind of advice.

On the very next pitch, the batter popped up, Mad Dog threw away his catcher's mask and caught the ball, then a commercial came on. It must have been the third out, Casey realized.

"Ah well," Missy chirped. "At least they're getting right on a plane after this and we won't have to deal with the tantrums if they lose."

"Tantrums?"

"Okay, not so much tantrums. Mine is more prone to sulks. Tyler...well, you never can tell with Tyler."

"Oh." Casey hadn't really thought about it, but she supposed that was the baseball player's equivalent of the bad day at work. Only they got to have it in front of tens of thousands of people, live on television, then have it analyzed in the news the next day. "God, I'm glad when I fuck up at work there isn't a press corps covering my every move."

That made Missy snigger and they got talking about various writers Missy knew, some of whom she liked, some she didn't, and so it was somewhat surprising when one of the writers she liked walked in a few minutes later.

"Here for some coffee, Ken?" she teased, as he made a beeline for the coffee set-up.

"God, yes, it's freezing out there. And now we're in rain delay. Crazy Boston weather."

"We are?" They all looked back at the television, which was showing commercials again.

"Ken, this is my friend Casey. We came up here to get out of the cold."

Casey shook his hand. He was wearing a button-down shirt and a pullover sweater vest and was going gray around the edges of his hair. "Nice to meet you."

"Ken, your honest opinion," Missy said suddenly. "Is Tyler

out of his mind? Was that whole thing with the leadoff batter an act? Or is he losing it?"

"Let me get some popcorn and we can discuss it, since now I've got at least a half-hour to kill even if the rain stops this minute." He filled a bag to overflowing using a big metal scoop, then showered the bag with some kind of salt and carried it back the table.

"Okay, is he crazy?" Ken repeated. "Yes, but that's not news. I think they were just playing with Hernandez, who's fast and can bunt for a hit, but green. He's only been up for like a week..."

Casey didn't understand a lot of what was said after that, as the two of them chatted about pitching in fairly detailed terms. But it seemed to corroborate a lot of what she'd picked up from the papers, too. Tyler hadn't been having a good year so far. He'd lost his first four starts of the year in a row, at least partly due to some fluke bad luck, then had won his last game, the game Casey had come to. If he lost this one, he'd be not only on his way to a terrible record, but he'd be in the doghouse with the fans and the team, too.

More writers came in as the delay stretched on, and soon it was like a small cocktail party, except everyone was drinking coffee and eating popcorn. Then a bit after that, a very gray-haired man in a wrinkled suit jacket burst in. All the writers looked at him as if he were a person of some importance.

"Sleet," he announced. "Ice pellets. The end times are nigh."

A hearty cheer went up from the writers.

❧

It was another two hours before the game was called off officially and Ken shook Missy's hand and said, "Well, I guess Hammond's luck had to change sometime."

Casey was surprised. "What? Didn't he lose 3-2?"

Missy stood up. "No. The rainout rolls the score back to the end of the last full inning. That three-run bomb doesn't count now. And because he pitched the full five innings, it's considered an official game, so he got lucky, all right."

"That's awesome." Casey wondered what Tyler would say about it. She supposed she could read about it in the paper in the morning.

Or she could call him when she got back to the apartment.

It was late but she didn't feel like sleeping, so she called his cell phone. "Hey, they tell me you got lucky."

"Hey, yeah, but I'll take it. Makes up for some of the bullshit losses from last month." He sounded tired. "We're about to get on the plane but I can call you back once we sit down."

"No, that's all right," she said. "I gotta crash now anyway. I just...oh, God, this is going to sound so corny, but...I actually just wanted to hear your voice."

"Well, thank God for the cell phone then," he said. "Hey, I'll see you in the city. You take care until then."

"I will."

After all, Thursday was only four days away.

CHAPTER FOUR

Casey arrived at the hotel around lunchtime. She'd had a nice ride on the Amtrak train into the city, and Tyler was standing in the lobby waiting for her when she came in. He had his sunglasses on, and was wearing a sport coat, which she didn't expect.

"There you are," he said, tucking his cell phone away and twirling her into a hug. "Right on time. Want to go grab something to eat? There's everything here, of course. Oh, wait, let's put your bag away first."

"All right." She would have been content to carry it if he'd wanted to go right then; it was just a backpack with one change of clothes and some toiletries. But she figured she might as well leave it off. They rode the elevator up to a small but nice-looking suite, the bedroom separated from the sitting room by a set of French doors. She plopped the bag on the couch. "Where do you want to go?"

"Everywhere!" he said, throwing his arms wide. "Off days are so rare, and off days that aren't spent packing to go somewhere are even rarer. I'm glad this worked out." He held out his arm for her and she took it as they went back to the elevator. "Today I get to pretend to be a normal person. Let's go to Times Square, eh?"

"Sure." It wasn't Casey's first trip to the city, or Tyler's either, but there was something about New York that made each visit new, and yet the same. They ate in a Thai restaurant they stumbled across on one of the side streets a few blocks from the hotel, then wandered through the throngs of spring tourists in Times Square. Tyler haggled with a street vendor over buying an "I Love New York" T-shirt, and Casey wasn't quite sure how it happened, but it ended up with him buying an entire case of the shirts for about fifty bucks, and some kid on a bicycle trundling off to the hotel with the box strapped on the back with bungee cords.

"That was totally like...Third World," she said, watching the kid struggle to pedal away.

"Yeah, wasn't it?" he said, putting his sunglasses back on. "I went on this good will baseball tour to China when I was in college, saw a lot of stuff like that."

The question was out of her mouth before she had a chance to wonder whether she cared about the answer. "Oh? Where'd you go to school?" *Stupid. Asking him about the trip to China would probably be better.*

"Oh, University of Texas, for the baseball program, of course. Couple of places tried to recruit me. I picked the one with the warmest weather."

They moved on through the crowd, past a giant toy store with a small Ferris wheel inside it. "I never finished. Once I got drafted, I didn't go back. They say I still could when my career's over, but can you imagine me at forty years old, sitting in a classroom with a pencil behind my ear trying to do algebra or something? Doesn't seem likely. And it's not like I need a college degree or I'll end up scrubbing floors somewhere. Or selling T-shirts and electronics on the street."

She nodded, wondering if she should be avoiding the subject of salaries and money, or if those rules didn't really apply, when she'd read in *The New York Times* online that he was making $10.5 million this year. "So where to now?"

"You want to see if we can get tickets to a show or something? *Phantom of the Opera*? Man, it's so weird not to have a game."

Casey hooked her arm through his as they walked. "Don't you get a couple of months off, though, in the winter?"

"Yeah, but once the season starts...you just have to be in the mentality that there's a game every night. If you wish you had days off, you won't be mentally ready to play. But then it feels weird when you don't have a game, like you're skipping school or something."

"But I thought you only played every fifth day anyway."

"Yeah." He shrugged. "But there are things I do on each day between starts, part of my program to get ready for the next start. Kind of like how football teams have stuff they do all week between games, except I'm just one guy. The rest of the team has to go out and play every night. You just...you get kind of addicted to it, almost, and then you miss it when it's not there, even just for one night."

He stopped walking then and turned to face her. "But don't get me wrong. Having an evening out with you is...I've been thinking about it all week. So what do you think? Broadway show?"

"Do you think we can still get tickets this late?"

"Hang on." He took his cell phone out of his pocket and

dialed. "Hi, yes, this is Tyler Hammond in room 1253. Heh, yeah, thanks. I was wondering, what are the chances you could get me two tickets to...uh..." He motioned to Casey to say something.

Casey racked her brains trying to think of a show she wanted to see. "*Chicago?*"

"*Chicago,*" he said into the phone. "For tonight. Oh, that would be awesome. Great. Call me back if there are any problems. Yeah." He gave his number and hung up. "God, concierges are great."

She grinned. "I wish I had one in everyday life."

He laughed nervously. "Uh, yeah."

"Tyler, what's wrong?"

"I'm embarrassed to admit I do actually have one. A concierge desk, I mean. I'd never have stuff from the dry cleaners in time or anything without them." He was actually blushing.

"Is that a bad thing?"

"I just didn't want you to think I was lazy."

She punched him in the arm and they went back to walking. "So the show's not until later. What should we do until then?"

"We could take a boat tour to see the Statue of Liberty, we could go up the Empire State Building, we could go to a museum. They have dinosaurs at one of them, don't they? Or the planetarium. There's supposedly fun shopping in Greenwich Village..."

Casey laughed. "You sound like you'd rather see the dinosaurs than shop."

"Well, that's true..."

"Can we just hail a cab and say 'Take us to the dinosaurs?'"

"Probably."

༄

Four hours later ,they had seen the dinosaurs at the Museum of Natural History and ridden a horse cart through Central Park, during which ride the carriage driver had told Tyler he needed to come play for the Yankees. He outlined all his points, including how the Yankees were surely going to be the ones to offer him the most in free agency, had the most players in the Hall of Fame, and so on. Tyler had demurred, saying that was all in the future and right now, he wasn't even in the American League.

That prompted Casey to finally ask what was up with the leagues. She understood there were two separate leagues, the American League and the National League, going way back to the dawn of the 20th century. "But I looked at the schedule and you play some of the American League teams."

"Yeah, they've been doing that for years now. Inter-league play. It means we'll get to play the Red Sox later in the summer. That'll be fun, won't it? Boston is such a sports-crazed town. They'll have to declare martial law to keep people from rioting." Even though the Robins had only moved into Boston a short time ago, they already had quite a following. "What do you say, buddy? If I sign with the Red Sox, I won't even have to move."

"Man, the Red Sox suck," is all the driver would say to that.

They then rode the subway down to Soho and Casey

convinced Tyler to come with her into some art galleries, and he even seemed to like some of the cool modern art she showed him. "Yeah, when I think art, I think of paintings of vases of flowers and fat women," he said, without any trace of meanness. "But this stuff is cool. I think I like the sculptures the best."

Casey was tempted by a sculpture that looked a bit like a giant crescent moon, only it was iridescent colors, made of metal with a pitted and scarred surface. On its chest-high pedestal it stood as tall as Tyler, a grand almost-circle almost like the horns of a great ox. She looked at the price tag. Not only would the piece be totally out of place in her rundown apartment, it cost easily a third of her annual salary after taxes.

The gallery owner chatted with her about the piece anyway. "God, it's really beautiful. I really like it, but I don't have room for something like this in my tiny apartment," she said, trying not to mention that it was priced light years out of her reach.

Tyler came up behind her, steering her aside from the owner. "But it'd look great in my ultra-modern place, wouldn't it?"

"Yeah, with those huge ceiling you have and the...wait, you're not thinking of buying it, are you?"

"I want to buy it for you, but you can keep it at my place, and you know, visit it there. Until you move somewhere bigger, eventually. Right? After you learn to play golf and get into management?"

She groaned. "You can't buy me something that expensive."

"Why not? I bought my mother an entire house and two cars. It's not like I'm going hungry, right? What's money for?"

She looked up at him and he looked really earnest, like if she said no, he might actually be hurt. "Are you sure?"

"Are *you* sure?" he asked back. "If you really like it, it's yours."

Her palms were starting to sweat. "Yeah. I really like it."

"Awesome. It's going to look so cool in the sitting room. I'll have to invite people over on the next off day at home for cocktails to look at it." He grinned like a boy getting a new puppy. "Uh, miss? Ma'am?" He flagged down the gallery owner and set about buying it and having it delivered.

Casey didn't listen to most of the details, just stared at the piece with a hand on her cheek, feeling it burn. But it was a pleasant burn.

When they went back out onto the street, Tyler was holding her hand. "You okay?"

"Yeah. I'm just kind of stunned."

He smiled. "Look. Whatever guy you go out with, each one has something different about him, right? One guy's maybe really handy with the fix-up stuff. One guy's maybe really smart and can, like, do your taxes for you, right? Well, you happen to be going out with a jock who makes more money than he knows what to do with, so, you know, this kind of thing happens."

She laughed at that. "Okay."

"So, what do you think it was a sculpture of?"

"Of? Well, I think it's supposed to be abstract. You interpret it how you want to. But I saw it as a kind of crescent moon. You know how sometimes it almost looks like it could go all the way around but it doesn't? That's what it made me think of."

"That's really cool. Now I really think we should grab a

snack before the show, and just have a late dinner after. Maybe room service. Got to love the twenty-four-hour room service. It's half the reason the team stays where it does."

"Sounds good to me."

They were walking back to the hotel from the theater when Casey put her arm around Tyler's waist, pulling him close as they walked in step with each other. He smelled more like aftershave than she usually preferred, but under it she could still tell it was him, just a hint of something that reminded her body of how his skin tasted. It was a nice feeling, wanting him, and not feeling either guilty or pressured about it. It just felt, well, nice.

"Are you having a good time?" he asked as they turned the corner into a stiff Manhattan wind.

"A terrific time."

"I'm not just an excuse to get away from the office?" He grinned.

"And what if you are? Going to kick me out of bed?" She grinned right back.

"No, ma'am," he said with a raised eyebrow. "So I guess I know what we're doing when we get back to the room?"

"Unless you have a better idea," Casey said, half daring him to suggest something.

But that was the end of the jokes. He pulled her into a hug, and she could hear the satin lining of his sport coat hissing against his other clothes as he enveloped her in his arms. "I'm glad."

"About what?" she asked, looking up at him.

"Mm, just, you know, some girls wouldn't be so nice to me."

Casey didn't really understand that comment, but she wasn't about to start trying to pick it apart now. Maybe she could ask Missy a bit about Tyler's previous girlfriends next time she saw her. Nice to him? What was the point of going out with a man who was the epitome of sex on wheels, then holding out on him? Maybe some of them really only wanted him for his money? That seemed quite possible.

She slipped her hands into his trouser pockets and felt not very subtly for his erection. He was only half hard, but as her fingertips brushed him, she felt him stiffening. She kept touching him until it seemed he was fully hard and he groaned.

"Soooo nice to me," he said.

"Just be nice back," she said and stepped back and tapped him on the nose. "Come on."

In the lobby, they ran into Mad Dog and a few of Tyler's other teammates. He introduced her to Madison, and Casey shook his hand, finding it huge and rough. "I've met your wife," she said. "In the stands. She's great."

"Isn't she, though?" Mad Dog said. He glanced at Tyler, seemed to read something there, before adding, "If you come on more road trips, I'll try to get her to come along, too. You guys can hang out."

"Sure." She gently pulled at Tyler's hand then, trying to be obvious without being too obvious about wanting to go upstairs *now*.

"Don't stay up too late," Mad Dog said to Tyler as they

were walking away. "Big start tomorrow."

"Yeah, yeah," Tyler said, and pulled Casey into an open elevator. "Ignore him. Catchers always think it's their job to nursemaid pitchers."

Casey looked at him. "Should we not stay up too late, though?"

He snorted. "The early bus to the park doesn't leave here until two thirty in the afternoon. I think we'll manage. It's not even eleven now, is it?"

"Nope."

In the room, they discovered a cheese plate, a bottle of champagne, and note from the reservations manager saying, "Go Robins!" Tyler eyed it suspiciously. "Okay, now, see, if it were the night after I pitched, and I won, then it might be okay. But it might all be a ploy on the part of some Mets fan to put me off my game tomorrow."

She sniffed the cheese. "Well, why don't we just save it for tomorrow? If we keep it in the ice bucket, they won't throw it away. We can stick the cheese plate in the mini bar and test it for contamination later."

He laughed. "All right."

Casey put the plate away, tucking it into the mini bar on top of the jarred peanuts. Then she drifted into the bathroom and brushed her hair, which had gotten a bit tangled in the wind. She knew Tyler was watching her as he went to hang up his sport coat and take off his shoes.

She was suddenly nervous, butterflies in her stomach. How was it going to go this time? Was it going to be as good as before? She was *really, really* starting to like him.

He came up behind her then, lifting her hair to press a kiss against her neck. "Now if I remember right, you have a spot," he said, his lips brushing her skin as he talked, "somewhere, right about...here..."

She pressed back against him with a gasp as his tongue found that place that seemed connected directly to her clit. She wondered what that warm velvet would feel like down there and she moaned aloud.

"Bed now," she said.

"You sure?" He moved to the other side, lips and tongue searching for the matching spot there, his hands on his hips and the firm press of his erection against her backside. "You sure I shouldn't just lift you up on the bathroom counter here and slip it in you?"

She moaned again, not knowing whether he meant to do it or just use the idea to arouse. His hand slipped around to the front of her, grazing over her mound with light pressure.

"I can make you come just as many times in here, you know..."

"Bed," she said more firmly, then squealed with laughter as he lifted her up with another "yes, ma'am" and carried her through the French doors to the enormous bed. He half-tossed her onto it so she bounced a little, then started dragging her pants and panties down. He got one leg free of her clothes and then put his shoulder under the bend of her knee, pushing her onto her back and spreading her legs.

One of his hands spread her lips gently and then she felt a long, slow swipe of his tongue up one side of her labia. It was too deliberate for him to have just accidentally missed her clit. Then he did the other side and she groaned, grinding her hips toward his face.

"Now now," he scolded. "You know it'll be better if you let me take my time." He bent his head again, this time flicking his tongue butterfly light all around her clit, but still not touching it directly except for the occasional brush.

She chuckled inwardly. Sex, and maybe Tyler, too, was a pile of contradictions. He was in such a hurry to go slowly that he hadn't even taken her pants all the way off, or even touched her shirt. Just went straight for the "good part." And yet it didn't feel like he was rushing or neglecting her at all, the way it might have with another guy.

His tongue snaked over her clit and she gave a long moan. That was the funny thing, she thought. The guys who were in the biggest hurry were the ones who really didn't know how to turn her on like this. She was completely ready for Tyler to fuck the living daylights out of her after just that little bit—she was ready even back in the bathroom. But when was the last time she'd spent all day with a guy thinking about, and knowing, they were going to have sex that night?

He brought her all the way to the edge of orgasm with his tongue, then eased her back down to a lower plateau of pleasure before lifting his head, his chin glistening. "So, you want to come now? Or you want me in you like last time?"

"Um..."

"Or there's this..." he said, waggling his eyebrows as he slipped a finger into her and tickled her g-spot.

"Hey!"

"Too much? Don't like it?" He continued to touch it, but with a lighter pressure.

"N-no, I love it, I just...oh...." He did something else inside her then, with two fingers it felt like, and her eyes rolled back in her head and she arched her back. "Oh fuck, you could pretty much make me come just from that."

"Really? That would be so awesome. I've never made a

girl come just from, you know, being in her. Well, I *might* have once or twice, but I'm pretty sure they were faking."

"Well, I've never come just from something in me, but..." She bore down on his fingers again. "But God, it feels good when you lick me, too."

"That sounds like a hint," he said, and went back to licking her while doing what he was doing with his fingers.

Casey came within seconds, crying out loudly and clawing at the pillows. When she had fallen limp and panting, he lifted his head again. "That's what I'm talking about."

"What?"

"It's just a catch phrase. You are awesome."

She laughed. "I think I'm supposed to be the one saying that now."

"Here, say it to this." He slipped his pants off finally and reared up on his knees, his cock riding high and full.

She put a hand under his balls the way you would the chin of a big dog before talking to it. "Hmm, I dunno. Your cock's awesomeness has yet to be proven tonight."

He made an affronted noise. "Well, then! I guess I better get to proving it. Which way do you want it? Front, back, upside down, or all of the above?"

"Just come here," she said, kicking off her pants and pulling him between her legs. While she was at it, she stripped off her shirt and went to work on his. He finished it for her, then bent to leave kisses across the tops of her breasts.

"You ready now?" he asked. "I think you're forgetting something."

She blinked up at him. "Holy shit, you're right."

"It's okay, darling. I've got it." He had to get off the bed to retrieve the condom, but he returned quickly with it already in place. "There you go."

Casey just nodded. She was on the pill, so it wasn't like she was worried about pregnancy. But this was only their second date, and if Tyler's reputation was what it was, then it was better to be safe. She was grateful. Most guys would have just plunged in if she'd pulled at them like that, she thought.

"Impatient," she said, raising her eyebrow.

"Okay." His eyes were open and looking into hers as he entered her, a flicker of amazement in them as he slipped all the way in, his mouth slightly open as if in surprise.

Her own expression mirrored his. She felt like she should say something, something that would capture the moment and burn it in her memory, but there were no words. Well, maybe one. "Good."

"Yes," he agreed, and he began to move inside her.

Chapter Five

The next day, Tyler pitched against the Mets and won. They had sex again that night, and Casey unexpectedly discovered that the thing that soothed the soreness inside her was more sex. Kind of like how sore muscles felt better with exercise, she figured. Riding the train back to Boston the next day, she pondered it. She'd never had sex for so long that she even got sore in the first place, but comparing Tyler to her previous lovers was like comparing a racehorse to pony rides. He was in terrific shape, of course, so had a ton of stamina, and he didn't seem like he was ever rushing to the end. He enjoyed the act itself, not just the result.

And his cock was bigger than she was used to, too. She squirmed a bit in her seat as little sensory flashbacks wracked her. Was there such a thing as too much sex? She really would have liked to stay one more night, and she nearly had, but she decided to stick to her original plan to go back on Saturday so she could walk with her company's group in a fundraising walk. Was it cystic fibrosis? Muscular dystrophy? She couldn't remember which now. She'd turned in her forms weeks ago after haranguing all her neighbors to sponsor her, so she figured she had better show up and actually walk the three miles or whatever it was. Plus, her boss was expecting her.

She had a promise from Tyler that they'd get together on Tuesday night.

"I thought the team wasn't coming back until late Tuesday, though," she'd said. "Flying back after the game."

"Yeah, but I'm pitching Wednesday. They send the starting pitcher ahead so we can be well rested."

"But if you see me, you won't be well rested," she had teased.

"Oh, but I will," he'd said, pulling her into a warm hug. "I sleep so much better with you in the bed."

It wasn't just the sex that made her feel good. It was the things he said. The things he did. She stared out the window for the whole train ride, not really seeing all of Connecticut going by, just thinking about him.

Tuesday couldn't come fast enough. The walk left her with blisters on her feet and Monday at work was hellish. A major client left. It wasn't someone Casey worked with directly, but it put everyone in a sour mood, and it became one of those days where each thing she started got interrupted by something else, so that by the end of the day, nothing was done. Tuesday was barely better, though at least she knocked a few things off the to-do list, meaning she felt only the tiniest bit guilty when she left at five fifteen, sneaking out while her boss was on a conference call with someone on the West Coast.

She put on the sunglasses Tyler had bought her over the weekend and came out of the elevator on the ground floor into the bright glassed-in lobby full of sun. A pair of strong arms suddenly grabbed her from behind and twirled her in a circle before she could get scared. "Tyler!"

"Casey!" he answered, echoing her delighted and surprised tone just for fun.

"What are you doing here? I thought we were going to meet at your place at eight."

"We were, but I was running an errand and figured I'd wait around for you here." He shrugged.

"How long have you been standing here? I was lucky to get out when I did."

"Not long," he said, but it really sounded like he was lying. "Can I kiss you here?"

She glanced around. People were walking every which way and not paying them any attention. "Sure."

"Good." He bent and pulled her into a gentle kiss, running one thumb along the soft hairs on her neck. When he spoke again, he still held her close. "I was afraid if you showed up at my place at eight, I'd pounce you right then and we'd never get out to eat or anything."

Casey's breath caught. "I think that would have been fine."

"Let's at least get a snack first."

Casey could feel him right through all their clothes, pressing against her. "Are you sure you can wait?" She could feel herself melting inside, her body responding to him.

"You're worth the wait," he said.

They walked across the Common, hand in hand, Casey peripherally aware of people's heads turning when they recognized Tyler. He took her to a little Mexican joint that had a lively bar with twenty kinds of margaritas, but it wasn't necessary to drink. She felt giddy already just being with him. They sat in a corner booth, side by side, facing the back wall rather than the door when Tyler explained they'd be more likely to be left alone that way.

After they ordered and were waiting for their food, Casey realized he hadn't stopped touching her hardly at all since that first hug by the elevator. She grinned, liking both the attention and the affection. Such a simple thing. Why weren't other guys like that? His thumb brushed up and down behind her ear and it began to feel as if he were touching her somewhere more intimate. Goosebumps spread over her arms and she moved closer to him, squeezing his thigh with one hand.

"So, how was work?" he asked casually.

"Awful. But you really don't want to hear about that, do you? How was play?"

He laughed. "Hey, my job is work, too."

"Yes, but for *work* you 'play' baseball. So, how was play?"

"Awesome. Well, you know that. I won in New York. Tomorrow we play the Phillies and there's a good chance I'll win again. Are you going to come to the game?"

"I will if you want me to."

"I want you to."

"If you win, maybe I'll even congratulate you."

"Oh, how, with like a lap dance or something?"

"Yeah, sure." She laughed. "I'll tell them at work I have a doctor's appointment so I'll be in late. How's that?"

He grinned. "Well, then I'd better win, so it'll be worth it for you."

"Yeah, you' better. Because..." Wait, she couldn't actually say that could she?

He nuzzled in her ear. "Because what, Case?"

"Nothing." She felt her cheeks go hot, but it was a delicious feeling.

"That doesn't sound like nothing."

"Yeah, well." She nuzzled in his ear now, so she could tell him. The bar was noisy, no one would hear what she said anyway, but..."I want to have sex with you two days in a row for a reason."

"Go on, this sounds good."

"Well, you know you're kind of well endowed and so when we do it, I get sore. But over the weekend, I learned something important."

"Yeah?"

"Yeah. The thing that feels best when I'm sore like that? More sex."

"Yeah?" His voice went up with surprise. "But then what will you do on the third day, when I'm not around?"

"Hmm, good question. Maybe I'll have to buy a vibrator."

"Oh no, I don't like that idea at all," he said playfully. "I want to be the only thing in you."

"Keep talking like that and we're never going to make it through this meal."

"You're the one who brought it up..."

But just then the waitress brought them their food, and they disentangled themselves long enough to eat. Casey had a quesadilla, but Tyler's idea of a snack was a fairly huge burrito. She supposed that when you weighed two hundred pounds, but weren't at all fat, you probably needed to eat more to maintain weight than you did at her size.

She fed him triangles of her own meal, long strings of melted cheese pulling from his mouth to her hand. With Tyler, it seemed like just about anything could be foreplay. That was what made the meal bearable.

He left cash on the table so they wouldn't have to wait for

the credit card slip, and walked down the street toward his building.

They went into the lobby of the Ritz-Carlton and he pushed the button for the elevator.

"Wait a sec." Casey looked around. "Your apartment is in the residential tower of the Ritz?"

He looked at her blankly. "You didn't know that?"

"I didn't realize it. That first night, when we ate in the bar...well, and then we took the elevator that time from the private parking...I suppose I should have figured it out, but I hadn't."

"Yeah, well, it's...ritzy, you know?"

It was a lame joke, but they both laughed anyway and got into the elevator.

The moment the doors closed, he moved her hand to the bulge in his fly. "I'm crazy hard, given that all we've done is have dinner."

She rubbed him through the cloth, his groan sending a shiver down her spine. "I want you."

"That's why we get along so well," he said, groaning again as she squeezed him. "At this rate, we're not even going to make it to the bedroom."

"Sure we will," she said. "I'll race you there."

She had hit on a winning strategy there, of course, as any hint of athletic competition was irresistible to Tyler. She got a head start as he fiddled with his keys, but he caught her just at the door to the room, swept her up in his arms and tossed her onto the bed. Then it was a kind of wrestling match, as they fought with their own and each other's clothes. Casey was crawling toward the condom drawer as Tyler stripped her socks off, and then she was tearing open the package. Tyler obligingly lay back so she could roll it down over his quivering prick, and then his breath caught as she straddled him.

"You sure you don't need anything else?" he said as he slipped his fingers between her legs, then whistled when he felt how wet she was. "Okay, I guess not."

"Hold still," she said, and he steadied his cock with his hand.

She slipped down onto him and he let go, groaning and closing his eyes. She could feel every inch of him, rocking back and forth on her knees, controlling the depth and angle of the penetration herself. "God, sex has never felt so good," she said.

"Maybe I'm just the right shape for you," he said, looking up through hazy eyes.

"Mm, maybe." She settled her hands on his shoulders and rocked a little harder, feeling sparks now as each time she pushed him deeper into her. "Feels good no matter what position."

He just hummed in agreement, his hands fitting in the crook of her hips, thrusting upward into her. "Hold still. See how this feels."

She held herself just a few inches above him and he thrust up at a quick pace, making her moan. "Feels...incredible."

"Mm, glad to know all those ab crunches I do are good for something." But it was difficult to keep that up for more than a few minutes, and he pulled her down close again. "Have you tried side by side? Like this."

He was strong and limber, and moved her easily into position without ever pulling his cock all the way out, their legs interweaving and one of her legs ending up over his shoulder. Now he could still thrust with his hips, but one of his hands was free to roam the entire front of her body.

"You want to come with me in you?" he asked.

"Always," she answered.

"All right. I'll work on that," he said with a grin. His thumb brushed over her clit in time with his thrusts.

"That's not going to take long at all," she said, her voice coming out a breathy whisper.

"Plenty more where that comes from," he added, as he quickened his pace.

What a feeling. Her orgasm seemed to blossom from somewhere deep in her, shooting suddenly outward until her toes and fingers tingled, and tailing off slowly, oh so slowly, as he continued to thrust, now deep and slow. "God..."

"No, just Tyler," he whispered and kissed her. "What do you want next?"

She looked up at him. "Um, besides for you to just keep fucking me?"

"Yeah."

"Nothing. Want more of the same." Casey reached up and ran her thumb over his cheek. "You know what I've never done?"

"What?"

"Come just from fucking. I mean, without a hand or something on my clit. I'm not sure it's possible for me."

He raised an eyebrow. "We can try it. If it doesn't work, we can try something else."

"Okay. Missionary's probably best for that?"

"Yes, ma'am," he said, swinging her leg down and shifting them, again without ever pulling out. "How's this?"

"Feels good even if I don't come," she said, settling under his rhythm. "Mmm, more."

"You got it."

They fell silent then, the only sound their panting breaths and the rustling of their bodies against the bed covers. It felt incredible, and Casey felt herself moving gradually closer, infinitesimal steps toward completion. With other lovers, she wouldn't have believed they could get her there before getting tired or deciding she was too demanding, or too hard to please. But with Tyler, it didn't feel like that at all.

She felt herself tightening around him. He groaned and slowed. "Making it hard to hold back when you do that," he said. "Want to make it last for you."

"Close," she said. "Just...a little harder, a little faster. If...if you come, that's okay."

"If you say so..." He did as she asked, doubling his pace while she pulled at him, setting the rhythm she needed.

Oh, God. Oh God, yes, there it was, almost, almost, almost... If only she could get there before he did. "Tyler!" She shouted his name once, then a wordless cry as she came, gripping onto him with everything she had, every one of his thrusts pushing her more and more, higher and higher, until his groan joined hers, a last volley of quick thrusts announcing his own arrival.

"I'm sorry. I must be crushing you," the limp heap of man on top of her finally said.

"No, it's okay," she said, unable to contemplate moving just yet. "Stay in me as long as you can." She moaned as an aftershock shook her and sent a ripple through her, making him groan as she tightened around him again. Then came another one, this one forcing his soft cock from her.

He moved carefully to one side, and she was vaguely aware

of him taking the condom off as she drifted in a deep orgasmic haze.

"Yeah," she said, when he pulled a blanket over them and cuddled her close.

"Yeah," he agreed with a nod and a soft kiss. "And just think, it's only like eight o'clock now. We can do it again in a few hours."

"Awesome."

∽

"Girl, you are absolutely glowing," Missy said with a raised eyebrow, as Casey slipped into her seat just before the National Anthem. "Tyler must be treating you nice."

Casey thought her cheeks were probably glowing at that, as Missy's teasing made her blush. "Saw him last night, yeah. Plus this leaving the office at a decent time once in a while has felt pretty good, too." She'd had to leave tonight at six fifteen to make it to the game on time, and here she was, just barely making it before the first pitch.

They stood for the anthem, Missy singing along softly with one hand over her heart, then they sat back down again. "So how was the trip to New York?" Missy asked. "I should have gone, but it's not like they won't go again like three more times this year."

"Wonderful. We saw a Broadway show, did some shopping." Casey debated whether to mention Tyler had bought her a sculpture with a five-figure price tag on it, then installed it in his own apartment since hers was too small for it. She decided not to.

Out on the mound, Tyler was just starting his warm-up

pitches and she watched him while talking. "Are you going to go on the trip to Philadelphia in like two weeks?"

"Why, you want to go? Can you get the time off from work?"

"I *have* to take some time off because if I don't use up some of my vacation days, I'm going to lose them," Casey said. "But anyway, my folks are in the Philly area."

"Ahhh," Missy said, comprehending. "So are you going to introduce him to the family?"

"That's what I'm trying to figure out."

"Well, he won't, you know, chew on the leg of the table or embarrass you like that..."

"Yeah, I know. But if he turns out to be a summer fling? Or wants to be? My mother won't hesitate to come in with the marriage-and-kids questions if she's in the mood." Tyler stepped off the mound as Mad Dog threw the ball to second base. Casey paused while Missy shouted at her husband, then picked up again when Missy looked back at her. "We've only known each other for a month. I don't want my parents thinking I'm, like, a groupie or something."

Missy looked thoughtful. "Well, the mom interview might be tamped down somewhat by the fact that if you introduce them at the field, there won't be much chance to corner him alone. Hmm, except it's not that easy to get field passes at other stadiums. Although knowing Tyler, he probably could swing it. He knows everybody everywhere, it seems. But if you break up in a couple of months, will your parents think any differently about that than these guys you told me about who never last more than three dates?"

Casey slumped miserably in her chair. "I don't ever bother to tell her about them. Except after the fact, maybe."

"Well, does it feel like your thing with Tyler is near the end?"

"No! Oh no, not at all. Feels like we're still just getting started." Out on the field, the first batter took up his position, while Tyler pushed his hat down low over his eyes and glared at him. "It just feels so wide open, you know? Which is exciting, that I don't know where it's going. But it just complicates the issue of what to tell my family."

Missy touched her arm lightly. "You know, if it all goes wrong and you break up later, I don't think you have to tell your mom anything more than that you fell head over heels in love and then he broke your heart. She'll be on your side."

"I... but..." Casey watched as the batter went back to the dugout, having struck out on three pitches. "But I don't know if that's true."

"You mean, the head-over-heels part?"

"Yeah."

Missy looked at her. "Okay," she said slowly. "The point is, though, it'll be believable to your mom. Whether you actually fell for him or not, that's your business and she doesn't need to get into that."

"Huh. I never thought of it that way."

"What, telling your parents what they want to hear? Or what they expect to, anyway?"

"Yeah. I've always been more of the just don't tell them anything at all type. But that's getting tiresome, I guess." Casey fell silent, though, thinking about the head-over-heels comment.

As the Robins were leaving the field, she watched Tyler jog to the dugout. He looked up and waved in her general direction. She wasn't sure he could actually pick her out of the crowd this many rows back, but just the thought that he'd looked at her, for her, sent a jolt through her heart. "So," she said to Missy, once he'd disappeared under the roof of the dugout, "it really looks like I'm head over heels for him?"

"That's what it looks like," Missy said in a neutral voice. Then she saw her husband come out on deck. *"Come on, Madison! Get a hit!"*

They watched the game for a while, Missy explaining little points from time to time, but they didn't discuss Tyler again until the fourth inning.

"How's this for a plan?" Missy said, checking the calendar on her fancy cell phone. "You invite your parents to join us for dinner on Saturday after the game. It's a one o'clock game, so it'll all be over with and the boys will be cleaned up and back at the hotel by five, five thirty. Tell them Tyler and Mad Dog are taking us out somewhere fancy—pick the best restaurant in the city—and invite them to come along. John and I will help keep Tyler in line and having more of us there, you're probably not going to get the super private questions like you would if he went to eat at your folks' house, right? How's that sound?"

Casey thought it over. "It could work. My folks are foodies, so a fancy place works. I wonder if my brother is anywhere around? He used to be into baseball when he was a kid."

Missy laughed. "All American boys are into baseball at some point in their lives. But it won't matter. It's Tyler. He's going to be the star, the center of attention, no matter where he goes. Even if they've never heard of him, he'll dazzle."

"What do you mean?"

"Look at him out there, Case." Missy waved to the figure on the field, who at that moment was wandering around on the grass behind the mound, looking like he was talking to the baseball in his hand. "There's forty thousand people here, and a million watching on TV, and four umpires, and eight guys on his team, and a batter standing there waiting for him. Absolutely everyone is looking at him, and waiting for him, and he loves it."

Tyler picked up the rosin bag and threw it down in a white puff of dust, walked up the back side of the mound and back down, glared at the runner on first base, then waved for Madison to come out for a mound conference.

"The thing is, the pitcher holds the ball. Nothing happens until he throws it. He has everyone captivated by his every move, whether he scratches his ass or what." Missy chuckled. "Tyler loves that part about being a pitcher. He has no qualms at all about delaying the game, even when a million people are hanging on every thing he does."

In the end, he handed the ball to Madison, who gave it back to the umpire, who threw it out of play and tossed Tyler a new one. "What was that all about?" Casey asked.

"Who the hell knows?" Missy texted a note to someone on her phone. "There, I just left a message for John. He probably doesn't know either, though."

As it turned out, after the game, Tyler told the media that the balls tonight were "seditious," and were trying to leave the park. He didn't want them doing it via the home run, so he had some of them removed from play. Casey got a text from Missy that simply read: *Did I mention Tyler's a nutball? But he's yr nutball. Love ya.*

When she got home after a late dinner with Tyler at the bar in the Ritz, she sent an e-mail to her mother asking if they'd be in town because she might be coming down. She didn't say why.

The next day at work was so crazy she didn't have a chance to check her personal e-mail until after her boss had left. Her mom had written back to say yes, and also threw in the tidbit that Nick would be home by then for the summer. Great. Next, to check with Tyler about Missy's plan, then set it in motion.

She saw Tyler again on the weekend, and it didn't seem like the sex or ardor was going to cool off any time soon. He pitched the next day and won again, and since it was a weekend day game, they went out afterward and had sex again, then Casey slept late on Sunday at his place even though he had to get up to go to the ballpark.

The sculpture had been delivered, and she sat sipping a cup of coffee and wearing his bathrobe, looking at it. It still evoked the crescent moon to her, a sliver of something that suggested a larger whole.

Her phone beeped to tell her she had a text message and she went and dug it out of her purse. Missy again: *Shuttle flight's booked for Friday night. Want airport limo to get you from your office, or will you take the subway? Traffic is a bitch then.*

Meanwhile, her next date with Tyler was set for Wednesday night. "I've got an idea," he had said over the phone when they'd discussed it.

"What is it?"

"I'm pitching Thursday, getaway day."

"What?"

"That's what we call it when we have a day game instead of a night game so that the team can then travel on the same day. Getaway day. Anyway, Thursday's game is at one, so I'll have to get up early, but then so will you, it being a school night and all."

Casey laughed. Tyler always called it a "school night" when she had to work the next day. "Yeah, that's true."

"But you know, it's so hard to wait until the weekend all the time, especially with road trips, so...I was thinking it might be good for us to get together Wednesday night, early-ish, since we'll both be on an early schedule."

"What's your idea of early-ish?"

"Well, technically I can't leave the ballpark until like ten or so, but I can be home by ten thirty if I push it." His voice slowed down. "And I was think-ing..."

Casey felt a little thrill go through her. When Tyler was "think-ing" usually meant something pleasurable was in store. "Yeah?"

His voice was low. "Why don't you head over to my place around ten, get in bed and wait for me?"

She grinned. "Should I play with myself while I'm waiting for you? I could, you know, get myself nice and wet..." She was blushing furiously but still managed to be bold enough to say it.

He rewarded her with a groan. "Don't talk like that. You're making me hard."

"Your place Wednesday, then."

"Yessss."

So she was looking forward to this "early night," and she was tickled by the thought of them getting up for work in the morning together, imagining them like some working couples who would kiss each other goodbye at the train station as they went their separate ways. She pictured Tyler in a three-piece suit with a briefcase packed with a baseball glove and balls in it.

But around eight o'clock Wednesday night, she was still in the office when her cell phone rang. It was Missy's caller ID, so she picked it up.

"Case, I have bad news. Tyler's on his way to the hospital for X-rays, maybe an MRI."

"What?" Casey shut her office door and cradled the phone to her ear. "What happened?"

"I'm not sure. Apparently he slipped during team warm-ups tonight and pulled something or sprained something. John thinks maybe his ankle, I'm not sure. Anyway, the trainers have him and he told John to tell me to tell *you* he doesn't know when he'll be able to make it. In fact, if these things go the way they usually do, they won't be done with him for a while. I think they're only just now on the way to the hospital."

Casey sat down. "They really took him to the hospital?"

"Yeah. I guess he didn't think anything of it when he slipped, but it swelled up while he was sitting on the bench, and next thing you know, they're whisking him away. John's pissed. Tyler was probably horsing around while shagging flies or something, and here he had a five-game win streak going."

"Shagging what?"

Missy laughed, in spite of the serious topic of conversation. "You're right. Everything baseball players say sounds obscene. Shagging flies is what they call catching the fly balls in the outfield during batting practice. All the pitchers go out there and do it since they don't do fielding drills. Anyway, he's gone, and he urged John to tell me, so he sneaked up to his locker and called me, and now I'm calling you."

"Well, damn it," Casey said, not sure how to feel about it.

Sure, she was disappointed she wouldn't get to see him tonight, but more than that, she was worried he might be seriously hurt. "Is it bad enough, you think, to call off the trip to Philly?"

"Watch the news tonight before you go to bed, or check ESPN.com. I bet they'll say."

Now it was Casey's turn to laugh.

"What's so funny?" Missy asked.

"Nothing. It's just...how many people get to turn on the TV to find out how their boyfriend is doing?"

"Tch. Yeah. I'll talk to you later, hon. It's noisy here."

CHAPTER SIX

Casey hung up and packed up her laptop. She'd only stayed late because she'd planned to go straight to Tyler's without going home first. As it was now, she didn't feel like going home. She came out of the building and turned toward the Common and the train station, but then kept walking. Why not? She had never bothered to get cable at her apartment and surely ESPN would be the thing to watch to find out what was going on. And there was one place she knew would have a TV tuned to the channel.

She walked into the bar at the Ritz without seeing the *maitre d'* who had been so friendly to Tyler, but Hojo was there, pouring drinks. She settled herself on a stool, not sure what to say, and watched the ESPN headline ticker go by while she waited for him to come take her order.

As it turned out, she didn't have to say anything. "What can I...oh, hi, it was Katie, right? You came in with Hammond."

"Casey, but yeah," she said with a smile. "He got hurt, they said. Before the game. I wondered if there's been anything on ESPN."

"No shit," Hojo said, picking up the remote from by the cash register and bumping up the sound just a little on the screen showing Sportscenter. There were only five or six other people scattered throughout the lounge and he glanced at them guiltily, but none of them seemed to be noticing the change. The Robins game was on one of the other screens, but it was showing game action.

"So I guess you're still seeing him? Or are you here to, like, ambush him?" Hojo said as he poured her a club soda with a twist.

"Still seeing him," she said. "Why, have other women gone ballistic on him?"

He shrugged and set the drink on a napkin in front of her. "Not really. You're the first real person he's dated since he's been living here, though. And by real person I mean not a model or an actress or someone his agent fixed him up with for publicity purposes."

"How long has he been living here?"

"About two years? Ever since joining the Robins." He handed her the menu. "You hungry? Did they take him for X-rays or something?"

"Yes and yes," she said. "Give me some of those little dumpling things, and what's the soup today?"

"Low-carb dairy-free cauliflower bisque with lump crab-meat. No really, it tastes a lot better than it sounds."

"Sure, I'll try it." She handed the menu back and he keyed the order into the register. "Oh!" Tyler's picture had appeared on the flat screen.

But the announcer didn't say anything they didn't know.

Pitching star Tyler Hammond taken for medical tests, blah blah blah. She sighed. The next story was about a guy who looked familiar, too. Oh, right, Campbell, the big hitter that Tyler had fought with in that first game she had seen. Some kind of trade rumor involving him. Then the announcer switched to talking about tennis and Casey lost interest.

When Hojo brought her food, she asked, "So he really hasn't dated much?"

He shrugged. "Not that I've seen. Was that your first date that time he brought you here before?"

"Yeah."

"It was kind of nice he introduced you to us. I get the feeling we're sort of his family during the season, you know?"

And that made her think of another question. "Where does he live in the off season?"

"Florida, I think. He left for Thanksgiving, visited his folks and such, then after Christmas went down to work with a personal trainer for about six weeks. Then in mid-February, spring training starts and it goes until games start in April, which is when he came back." He checked the screen behind him, but the story was something about basketball. "What's the matter?"

She looked up from her soup. "Eh. Just thinking I really can't just take six weeks off to go hang out in Florida. But, well, that's months from now, so I shouldn't stress over it yet."

"Good plan," he said. "You sure you don't want something stronger? Or shall we wait to see if they tell us what's wrong with him?"

"Yeah, let's wait." Casey finished eating her food, then checked the time. The game was in the ninth inning. She texted him a quick message saying she hoped he was okay, but didn't tell him where she was. "You'd think he'd call."

"They don't allow cell phones in the hospital," Hojo said. "He's probably having an MRI or something. I had one after my bike accident last summer and it was like something out of *Star Trek*."

"What do you mean?"

"I mean it really looked like the set of a *Star Trek* episode, with this giant alien machine with a hole in the middle of it, which they then stick you into like you're some kind of science experiment, and it makes all kinds of loud noises. It's kind of scary for the first five minutes."

"What happens after the first five minutes?" Casey asked, confused.

"Oh, same thing, but it starts to get boring. Thank God they were only doing my knee, so it was just my leg in there, but still. It took like forty-five minutes. I'm just glad it wasn't my head in there."

They went on chatting that way for a while, Hojo describing the bike accident in grand detail. The game ended with a Robins win, Casey noticed.

It was almost midnight when Tyler limped in. His face went through three different shocked expressions when he saw Casey sitting there, ending with a laugh and a hug. "You are a sight for sore eyes."

"Or sore ankles?" she said.

"Oh God, I'm such a moron." He shifted himself carefully onto the barstool next to her. His entire foot was in a kind of high-tech cast. "Hojo, you been taking care of her? The usual for me, please."

The bartender lifted up the soda gun, but added, "You sure you don't want anything stronger?"

"God, with the stuff they gave me, I think alcohol would kill me. My leg locked up so they shot me with some kind of muscle relaxant...I had to leave my car at the park and take a cab because I'm not fit to drive as it is." He took the glass of soda water. "Anyway, the verdict is that hopefully it's nothing serious. Mild sprain, I'll probably be fine if they tape it up before my next start. But I won't be pitching tomorrow."

Casey took all that in. "And the trip to Philly?"

"Oh, definitely still on," he said. "It's not like they're sending me to Alabama for surgery or something." He let out a long breath, like he was only just now coming to a stop after running around. "Hey, I thought you had a meeting in the morning or something." He pulled Casey's hands into his lap.

"I do. But you're kind of more important than a meeting. Or sleep."

He smiled. "Do you want to go upstairs? Or was this really just a 'let's make sure Tyler's okay' visit?"

She looked up at him. "I do want to go upstairs. But you should rest and I do have a meeting. So I should go." *And I want to prove to myself I didn't just come here for the sex.*

He pulled her into a hug. "I knew I loved you for a reason. I'm going to totally crash right now then. But I'll see you Friday night at the hotel, right?"

"Yes. Missy and I are flying together."

"Oh, danger, Will Robinson! Don't drink too many nips in first class."

"First...?"

He clucked his tongue. "You don't think Missy booked you guys in coach, do you? I know it's only an hour flight, but come on. Wait, too expensive? Case, you gotta quit thinking about that. A plane ticket to Philly, even a first-class one, is like lunch money to me."

She frowned, but said, "Okay."

"No, really, not to disrespect your job or career or anything. But just let me pay for it, all right? My mother's like that, too. She still wants to change her own oil in her car. I'm like, 'Ma, I bought you a car that cost more than your house, don't screw with it.' But she'd rather do it than pay a few bucks to Jiffy Lube."

She'd never heard him talk about his parents before. Maybe his muscles weren't the only thing loosened up by the shot they gave him. "Where does she live?"

"Oh, she and my dad still live in Kalamazoo. They're separated now, but they only live like four miles apart—is that funny? She still has the house I grew up in and she doesn't want to move. I put a new roof on it and a new driveway, and built her a tennis court in the back, though. She's a big hit with her friends, has these Friday night tennis parties. It's awesome."

Casey smiled. "Will I get to meet her at some point, you think?"

"Oh, definitely, definitely. There's no team in Kalamazoo, of course. Let's think. We don't play Detroit, wrong league...um...yeah. She'll probably come here for a visit later in the summer, though. My dad, too, though they'll probably come at different times. Although you can never tell with them." He nearly slid off the stool, caught himself with a loud clack of the cast against the floor, then grimaced. "Okay, time for little Tyler to get in bed."

"Do you want help?"

He looked at her for a long moment. "You know what? No. Because you know exactly what is going to happen, or try to happen, if we go into that bedroom together. And I'm going to pass out, and it just won't be pretty. I'll get Jerry or one of the other guys to help me and make sure I don't fall down before I get there." He kissed her softly on the forehead. "Friday?"

"Friday."

He hobbled out, the broad-shouldered *maitre d'* Casey had met last time helping him.

Hojo and she exchanged a look. "I guess I need my check," she said.

He laughed. "Hammond's already paid it. He'd kill me if I charged you."

She shook her head, smiling. "All right. Let me at least leave a tip." She dug a five out of her purse and left it on the bar, then took a last few sips of her soda water.

As she made her way down to the lobby, the *maitre d'* caught up to her. "Casey?"

"Yeah, that's me," she said, surprised.

"I'm Jerry. Tyler was worried you'd missed the last train, so he sent me down with money for a cab for you."

"This is getting ridiculous," she said, even though Jerry didn't necessarily know what she was talking about. "I've got a job. I can pay for my own cab."

"Yeah, I'm sure you can," Jerry said. "But I can't just pocket this. You can give it back to him tomorrow if you want." He handed her a hundred-dollar bill.

"Yeah, okay."

Jerry put her into a cab and she paid the driver the whopping fifteen bucks that it took to get her to her apartment, and put the hundred into her jewelry box later, trying to decide if he had been serious when he'd said, "I knew I loved you for a reason."

THE HOT STREAK

⤫

Casey arrived at the airport slightly frazzled from the T getting stuck, but when she got there, she realized she didn't have to wait to check a bag. All she had was her small rolling suitcase and a first-class ticket already printed out, so she went straight to security. In the gate area she didn't see Missy anywhere though, so she picked up a magazine at the newsstand and sat down to read it by the windows.

She looked up as a familiar-looking woman sat down next to her. The woman saw her looking and stared back as if trying to place her, too.

"Lasagna," Casey said suddenly. "Shayna, was it?"

"Oh! Yes," the woman said, holding out her hand for a limp handshake. She looked like she still hadn't quite placed Casey. "Shayna McDowell."

"Casey Branigan." For some reason, she felt reasonably sure that adding "Tyler's girlfriend" wasn't going to get her much of a reception, and if Shayna hadn't remembered her connection to Missy, well, that was probably all right, too. "How's the cookbook coming along?"

"Oh, it's awful!" Shayna reached down into her tote bag and pulled out a somewhat dog-eared looking thing. "This is last year's. Isn't it cute? Pomona Wilks did the design and put it all together, but her husband just got traded to a West Coast team, so there you go. Now there's no one."

Casey looked at the "book" in her hands. It looked like it had been printed at a quick copy shop and spiral bound. Spiral bound was fine for a cookbook, but the cover was half falling off, and the drawing on the front wasn't very good. "Where did you have this printed?"

"Oh, I don't know. Someplace Pomona found. Michaela would know, since she wrote the check to them."

"Well, I'm a production manager at a design firm in town. I could probably help..." She was turning the thing over and over in her hands. They'd probably paid five bucks a pop to get it done at a Kinko's or something. "How many of them do you make?"

"Oh, gosh, I think we sold about a thousand of them last year."

"And the money's all for charity, right?"

"Yes, the Wives' Fund all goes to Children's Hospital."

"Can I ask how much you actually raised?"

"Oh, all total last year, about fifty grand, but the cookbook was only about ten thousand of that. A thousand at ten dollars each."

"Hmm." Casey did a quick calculation in her head. "I'm going to guess you sold the cookbook a few hundred at a time, so you got a few hundred printed at a time?"

"That's right."

"So you probably spend five thousand on printing alone. If you were selling the cookbook for ten bucks, but you paid five, then you only made five."

Shayna frowned at her as if she didn't like this news, or the messenger, much at all. "So what are you saying, that we should raise the price?"

"No, actually, if you're going to do a thousand anyway, I can probably get you a price closer to two dollars a book, and have it printed like a real book, with a four-color cover and everything. A *book* book."

Shayna brightened immediately. "A *book* book would be perfect! You can really do that?"

The Hot Streak

"You need a designer who can work with a professional printer. I can do that. What I'd need is for you to e-mail me all the actual recipes so I can do the layout. If we can get pictures from the team and stuff, I can have illustrations inside, all that kind of thing. And if it's fancy like that, you can probably charge more like fifteen dollars for the book. That's what people would expect to pay for it in the bookstore, right? So your five-thousand-dollar donation becomes more like twelve or thirteen thousand right there."

Casey didn't expect Shayna McDowell to hug her, but she did, seizing her suddenly and nearly choking her with her fur coat. "You're the best! You're amazing! Oh, quick, let me put your e-mail address into my phone."

They were just finishing exchanging contact information when Casey saw Missy hurrying toward them.

"Well, hello, gals," Missy said as she plopped down in the seat on the other side of Casey. "Shayna, I didn't know you were coming on this trip, too."

"Oh, yes, I'm thinking I'll try to make most of the weekend road trips this year."

"Good for you," Missy said, while Casey tried to figure out what she was missing in the conversation.

A little while later, Shayna went off to the ladies' room, and Missy put a hand on Casey's arm as she leaned a bit closer to say, "The reason she's decided to go on all the weekend road trips is that she busted Jim with a mistress last year."

"Oh jeez."

"Yeah. I don't feel *too* sorry for her, because she was a bitch before that, too. But what a dog, you know? I can understand the guys lapsing once in a while. There are always Annies around, take a tumble with a groupie or something, but a full-blown mistress who met up with him in all different cities? That's really shitty. And he couldn't really keep it a secret. It was one of the other wives who ratted him out, of course."

"Wow." Casey tried to picture it. What kind of woman would let herself be used that way, too?

"It gets worse. Shayna and the kids lived in Cincinnati where he used to play, and this mistress was in Boston, so he was literally like almost living a double life. It was like, hello, did you forget you have a wife and kids in another city? Man. So Shayna's put the kids in boarding school so she can be with Jimmy every day pretty much, trying to repair the marriage and all...that giant diamond on her choker? That was a big step in the repair process."

"You sound kind of skeptical."

"Yeah, well, it's none of my business, but if Doggy did something like that to me, I could give a damn about some diamond or whatever. But no one likes to see someone go through that. I used to like Jimmy McDowell, too. I didn't realize he was such a stupid fucker." She sighed. "Yeah, so, what were you guys talking about when I showed up?"

"Oh, I, um...looks like I'm taking over the cookbook."

"No way!" Missy turned in her seat to face Casey more directly. "What do you mean taking over?"

"Well, producing it. She said the woman who did it last year left because her husband got traded."

"What? Wilks? When?"

Casey held up her hands. "I don't know! That's what she said when she came in."

"Holy crap. It must have happened today. Damn, and Pomona was nice, too, if not particularly bright. So, you're going to do it?"

"Yeah. I always wanted to be a designer, you know? But it's so hard to break in. I do a little design in my current job, but most of what I do is herding cats. That is, making sure the actual designers and other people do what they are supposed to when they are supposed to." She sighed.

"Oh, wow, hang on." Missy whipped out her phone and dialed. Casey could hear the buzz of another line ringing briefly. "Damn, voice mail. Oh, wait, I know who'll know. I've still got Ken's number in here..."

She dialed again and this time someone picked up right away. "Ken! Missy. What's this about Wilks getting traded? We got who? Oh boy. Oh, this should be interesting. Yeah, we're at the airport now. Thanks, Ken."

She hung up and then looked at Casey. "You remember the big palooka that Tyler plunked in that first game you came to? Campbell? He's a Robin now."

Casey sat for a moment in stunned silence. "Wow." Then she smiled. "I wonder if his wife can cook."

The trade was the talk of the team, of course. By the time Missy and Casey got checked in at the hotel, the game was nearly over, and they were sitting in the bar waiting for the guys for only perhaps an hour before the first bus pulled up.

Tyler came gamboling over like an excited puppy when he saw Casey. "Hey! You're here!" He gave her a bear hug from behind while she was still on her bar stool. "Did you hear the news? Campbell's on his way here!"

"I heard," Casey said, turning in her stool so that she faced him. He put his hands on her knees. "But I thought you hated that guy."

Tyler snorted. "When he's on another team, yeah. But for us? He could be the missing piece. I'll looooove it when he hits home runs for *our* team."

"The missing piece?"

"Of the championship puzzle." Tyler was positively beaming. "Oh, and slight change of plans. I'm starting tomorrow."

"What? What about your ankle?"

"Well, it's better, pretty much. And with Wilks gone, the rotation got shuffled...it's me or call up some kid from Triple A."

Casey turned to Missy. "I'm picturing a tow truck."

"He means the minor leagues, hon," Missy explained.

"So, it's me," Tyler said, drawing himself up taller. "I'll be fine. They taped it up today in a way that made it feel good as new. But anyway, that shouldn't keep us from meeting your parents or anything, but if I win, well, we might not get the nicest reception everywhere we go. Just warning you."

Missy waved her hand. "I'm sure it'll be fine. They're not going to throw a cigarette in your soup at Morimoto."

Tyler blinked. "Where are we going?"

"A place my foodie parents picked out," Casey said. "Japanese fusion cuisine. The chef's very famous."

"Cool." Tyler grinned at her. "So did you guys eat already tonight? Or...?"

Casey grinned back. "Or what?"

He nuzzled her ear. "Or do you want to go upstairs and do it?"

She put her arms around his neck. "We can always call room service later."

"You have the best ideas." He slipped a hand under her knees and the next thing she knew, Casey had been literally swept off her feet. "Bye, Doggy, Missy! See you in the morning." And he carried Casey right out of the bar to the elevator. There he set her down and just held her hand. She couldn't help grinning like a kid. It wasn't just the sex. It was the feeling that Tyler simply couldn't wait to see her, couldn't wait to be with her, every time she saw him. And the fact that she felt exactly the same way.

They stripped quickly once they were in the room, and he kissed her up against the wall, rutting against her hip until he was completely hard. She then took his cock in hand and led him to the bed, pulling him along by it.

She lay down next to him, pressing her body along his length and stroking him with her hand.

"So what's your pleasure? Top, bottom, from behind?" he asked, brushing her hair back behind her ear.

"Let's talk," she said, looking into his eyes. She was trying not to sound too serious, but she was failing. "Just a little."

"Okay, sure," he said, propping himself on one elbow and pulling another pillow behind his head.

She kept stroking him. She wanted to just climb on and ride him until she came, but she knew she'd be thinking about some things that Missy had said the entire time if she didn't ask him about them now. "So what's the deal with 'Annies'?" she asked.

"Baseball groupies, you mean? Did Missy point them out to you in the lobby or something?"

"Yeah."

He shrugged. "They're, you know, just like groupies for rock stars and stuff. You're in a totally different class from them, you know."

"I know, but..." How to ask this? "But do you ever take

them up on their offers? I mean, some of them have to be kind of cute. And you know they're willing."

He winced. "Yeah, I hear what you're saying. But no, I don't do Annies, if that's what you're asking."

"Not even once in a while?"

"Phew. You ask the tough questions," he joked, arching into her hand, which was still caressing up and down his shaft. "You should get a job at ESPN. But seriously, no. I did once or twice when I was a rookie, but they're just not worth the trouble. Some of the guys really enjoy them, but some of them carry two cell phones, one with the number they give out to the Annies and one for their real wife or girlfriend."

"Holy crap, that's really...wow."

"Shitty, yeah, but...but men are dogs, you know that."

"Well, that's why I'm asking. Seriously, Tyler. I just want to know what to expect."

He took her hand in his then, removing it from his cock and holding it between his. "Casey. Since I met you, I haven't been interested in anyone else. I haven't had sex with anyone else, and I haven't even wanted to. I haven't even flirted with anyone else except maybe a waitress or two, but only to try to get better service, you know? And I know that's not my reputation and that this is going to sound like a line, but...but it's so true. I'm all about you right now, and I want it to stay that way, too."

She squeezed his fingers. "So when you get lonely on the road, you aren't tempted?"

He squeezed back. "It just makes me wish you were there more. If I'm horny, I've got a pretty strong right hand, you know."

She looked into his eyes. "Is that a promise, then?"

"Absolutely! No Annies, no sex with anybody but you, Casey. That's..." His eyes were a little misty-looking, she thought. "That's easy to promise because it's what I want. You. Just you."

She nodded. "Pretty easy for me to promise, too," she said. "Though it's not like I'm beating off offers like you are."

He kissed her fingertips. "It's still nice to hear."

"Okay, then. I promise it's you, only you, Tyler. In fact, since I know you're jealous of vibrators, too..." She moved their hands back down to their crotches. "How about I promise nothing goes inside me that you don't put there yourself?"

"Damn, Casey, that's hot." He slipped a finger between her lips and then made an appreciative sound when he discovered how wet she was. She bent one knee, encouraging him to explore more. He slipped a finger into her. "So, only what I put in?"

She nodded.

"You won't even finger yourself like this when you masturbate?" he asked, rubbing his fingertips against her g-spot.

"Nope," she said. "I'll just rub my clit. *In* there...that's your job."

"Yes, ma'am. I'll do my best to take good care of it." He crooked his fingers and she moaned with pleasure.

"You know what else I think?" she said, as he brought her close to the edge of orgasm. "If it's really just going to be you and me, you can forget the condom."

"Are you serious?" His eyes were round.

"I'm on the pill. And Missy told me the team docs checked you for STDs already." She raised an eyebrow.

"True, true. I just...wanted to be sure that you were sure."

"I'm sure. Come here." She rolled onto her back and pulled him after her.

He settled between her legs and she looked up at him as he began stroking his bare cock through her slick folds. "Where is it, where is it..." he said, raising an eyebrow at her. The head of his cock rubbed against her clit and she jumped a little. "There it is!"

He was holding himself up on his elbows, hips moving, rubbing her clit again and again with just the head of his cock. She'd never felt anything like it. No lover had ever even tried that. It was like his tongue, only smoother, and somehow a perfect fit.

"Good?" he asked in a whisper.

She could only nod, hoping he would keep doing it.

He did. Until she was close, so close, then changed his angle and began to dip the head of his cock into her, fucking her shallowly three or four times before slipping it up to rub against her again.

"God, that feels good..."

"Mm-hmm."

She could feel his thrusts getting deeper, but never all the way in, until she realized he was trying to hit her g-spot with his cock the way he had with his fingers. She bent her knees more, angling her hips, "Ahh!"

"There it is," he said again. "Eureka."

"God, yes..." It felt like soon it wouldn't matter what he did, her orgasm was building and the explosion was starting to feel inevitable. He kept alternating between her clit and inside her, back and forth, and soon she was hanging onto him with her arms, not even sure why, just pressing their chests together.

THE HOT STREAK

When he dipped his mouth to her neck and sought out that one spot with his tongue, she came, wrapping her legs around him and pulling herself onto him to get as deep a thrust as she could.

"Oh, jeez, fuck, Case..."

"Don't hold back," she said, already grinding against him, about to come for a second time.

"Gonna...gonna come inside you," he said, then groaned as he couldn't hold back anymore. She came a second time as he emptied into her with a series of quick, hard thrusts, then lay back, panting and staring at the ceiling.

"Oh my God, where'd you learn to fuck like that?" she exclaimed.

He flopped next to her. "Dunno. Just seemed like a good idea, you know? Originally, I mean. Now...well, I have had a little practice at it."

"Guess there's an advantage to a man who used to be a playboy," she said with a grin.

"That's right," he said, nuzzling close and then kissing her. "They were all just practice for you. And coming inside you is one of the hottest things I've ever done."

"You're the third guy ever," she answered, rolling onto her side so she could look into his eyes. "There was my first boyfriend when I was young and stupid, though I only let him the once. There was a guy a couple of years ago, once. And then there's you."

He chuckled. "I feel honored."

"You'll be the first to do it more than once, too," she said. "Maybe even tonight..."

"Oooh, nothing like giving a guy incentive," he said. "Just remember, I do have to pitch tomorrow."

She nodded. "I'll be on top so you can rest your arm. How's that?"

"Sounds like a deal."

CHAPTER SEVEN

Morimoto turned out to be an incredible restaurant. It looked to Casey like the set of a science fiction movie, with molded plastic everywhere and colored lights in the tables that would subtly shift the entire color of the restaurant from a lime green to a teal blue to a deep purple. The food was out of this world, too—beyond sushi, beyond nouvelle cuisine. Casey wasn't even sure half the time what she was eating, but it was all delicious and delightful. Tyler sat across from her, between her father and mother, while Madison sat between her father and her brother, Nick.

So far, so good, she thought, while they waited for dessert to come. Mad Dog had been surprisingly talkative, and he and Tyler had a few baseball stories they told in tandem which were both interesting and not too dirty for polite company. The mixture of company kept Casey's mom from grilling Tyler too much about embarrassing stuff.

That didn't stop her from hurrying into the ladies' room when Casey went, though.

THE HOT STREAK

"Boy, he's really a bundle of energy, isn't he?" Elaine Branigan said as she went into a stall. "Tyler, I mean."

Casey always thought it was a little odd to talk while peeing, but her mother always seemed to think it was okay, so therefore it must be okay, right? Still, she kept her replies minimal. "Yeah. Professional athlete, I guess."

"He seems really nice. He's trying really hard to impress your father, though."

"You think?"

"Oh, definitely. I have to ask, you know I do, Casey, how serious is this thing between you? I mean, are you really serious about someone who is such a celebrity?"

"Mom..."

"Not that I don't think you should enjoy it while it lasts, of course. You know how hard it is to get a table in here? I'm amazed. Utterly amazed. The hostess was telling us that one of the Japanese players on the team was here yesterday and they were giving us the same table that he'd had! But, you were saying?"

Casey finished up and was done washing her hands before she replied. "He doesn't seem that much like a celebrity to me," she said, as she checked her hair in the mirror. "I mean, with me, he's just Tyler. He doesn't act the way you'd think someone whose fame has gone to his head would."

"Well," her mother said, emerging and going to a sink herself. She then fluffed her own hair, which was short and salt and pepper. "He dotes on you, that much is clear, and honestly, dear, it's nice to see you with someone who interests you enough to pull you away from work."

"Mom, I'm really not that into this job."

"Which is why it's a shame you're such a workaholic,

wasting yourself on a job you don't love." She crossed her arms and looked at Casey in the mirror.

Casey sighed. Both her parents were academics, teaching at UPenn, and Casey was fairly sure they just didn't understand how "real" jobs worked. "I'm not a workaholic," she grumbled, but without much conviction.

Elaine pulled out a lipstick and touched up her makeup. "So do you think you'll still be with him at Christmas? Nick's girlfriend's parents have a condo in Aruba and they're asking if we might all like to go down there for the holiday. I know that's six months away, but those kind of trips need to be planned ahead."

"I—yeah. I don't know. I hope so. You didn't tell me Nick had a girlfriend, though."

"Caitlin. They seem serious enough to be trying to get us to meet her parents, anyway, so..." Her mother tucked the lipstick away and held the door open for her.

So, she seemed to be saying, *if your little brother can decide he's serious, you should be able to, too.*

Back at the table, they found the chef himself talking animatedly with the two ballplayers. "Ah, yes, yes! So many Japanese players are coming to America now. But it makes sense. If they really are the best in the world, they have to come here, to the toughest league, to prove themselves. It shouldn't matter where the talent comes from. If the major leagues are going to be the best league in the world, they should take the top talent from everywhere: Australia, Italy, wherever baseball talent can be found."

Mad Dog was sipping something from a tiny cup. "Especially if they can pitch. Pitching talent is the hardest to find. That's why so many good players come from the Dominican

Republic. They're so poor, they don't have video games and all that, so the kids just throw the ball around all day long. Their arms get strong."

Casey sipped from her own cup of grassy-tasting tea. Her father jumped in with a question about the food, and the conversation shifted from baseball to gourmet eating, and she caught Tyler looking at her and smiling a little smile.

That night, back at the hotel bar, they shared a nightcap with Ken, the writer whom Missy liked. Casey got the impression that the guy actually liked Tyler as a person and didn't just act nice to him for the sake of a story, which was probably why Missy approved of him. That didn't mean Ken didn't sometimes ask questions which sounded like they could have come right out of an ESPN interview, though.

"So you won today," Ken said, while they were waiting for their drinks to come, "and that makes six...no, seven starts in a row that the team has won, and that you've picked up the win, too. That's starting to be an impressive streak."

Tyler grinned. "It's just the law of averages, Ken. I had lost, what, five in a row before the winning streak started? And I wasn't pitching worse than I am now, was I?"

"Well, actually, your batting average against balls in play was pretty terrible in April and May," Ken said.

"Translate?" Casey whispered to Missy.

"See, that's what I mean," Tyler said. "That's so not in my control. I really think that's luck."

Missy turned to Casey. "He's saying that on balls that batters hit, you know how sometimes the ball will go in just the right place to get through the infield, whereas other times it goes right to a guy? He's saying that in April and May, for whatever reason, more of those balls were getting by, whereas now they're turning into outs. Tyler's not doing anything different. He's just luckier now."

"I'd rather be lucky than good," Tyler said, taking his drink from the waitress as she handed them around. "Plenty of guys who are good have bad luck and don't get anywhere."

"I'd rather be lucky *and* good," said Mad Dog, raising his glass.

"Hear, hear," Tyler agreed, and they all clinked glasses together. Casey smiled. Everything seemed to be going so well.

∽

It wasn't until the next morning, as she was getting ready to leave for the airport and Tyler was getting ready to go back to the ballpark, that things started to go wrong. She was just putting her things back into her suitcase when Tyler came and put his arms around her. "So what are the chances you could take off and come see me in Atlanta?"

She turned and put her arms around his waist. "When is that? I know I want to try to get to Chicago."

"Mmm. Atlanta's this coming Thursday. We're flying there right from here. Could you come down Wednesday? They're flying me ahead again, so I'll be rested up for Thursday's start."

"Tyler, you mean three days from today? I can't do that. I have meetings on Thursday morning that I need to be there for."

He nuzzled in her hair, taking a deep breath. "I won't have

anyone who loves me there to watch me," he said. "And they hate my guts in Atlanta for some reason."

She pulled back a little. "You're a big boy. I'm sure you can handle it." Then she frowned. He was looking really pretty stricken. "Can't you?"

He chewed his lip and looked into her eyes. "It'd really, really, *really* mean a lot to me if you were there," he said softly. "They do this thing there, the Tomahawk Chop, it's like the whole crowd wants to scalp you."

She sighed. "Tyler, they're just sports fans. You'll have Mad Dog and the whole team there. And I don't know if I want to sit with a bunch of bloodthirsty Indians fans."

"Braves fans," he corrected her. "But..."

"I can't go with you on every road trip," she pointed out. "There's that trip coming up where you're doing San Francisco, L.A., and Arizona, you'll be gone for like two weeks. I can't just tag along to every city."

He looked absolutely crestfallen. "I know," he said, voice small. "But I'd really like it if you could come to Atlanta. Your meetings are in the morning? Could you go to them, then hop a flight at about three in the afternoon? I'll pay for it, you know. I bet you could see the game, then hop a Delta flight back around eleven at night..."

"And not get to Logan until two in the morning and have to be at work at nine the next day?"

"Well, yeah...but wouldn't it be fun?"

She sighed. "It would be fun, but..." Casey bit her lip. If it was really only about the sex for her, then she shouldn't be interested in this jaunt, right? Whereas if there was something more going on, shouldn't she be trying to support her partner? "It's really that important to you that I'm there?"

He took her hands in his. "Yes. Yes, it really is. I know Missy won't be there, so you'll have to sit by yourself...oh, I know, I can probably get you into one of the luxury boxes. Would that be okay?"

"Tyler, where I sit really doesn't matter to me." She shook her head. "I can't believe I'm considering this." But wasn't Tyler more important than her job? Her mother's words in the ladies room were still stinging a little. "I don't know how much I can push my luck at my job."

"You've had to leave at two o'clock before, haven't you? Doctor's appointment or that sort of thing?"

"Well, yes, but usually I know a bit farther in advance. But..." She looked up at him, weighing the thought some more. "All right. I'll see if I can get a flight that works. If I can't, though, I'm not coming."

"Great! Take my AmEx number down so you can book it!" He spun her around and kissed her. "Oh my God, you've just made me so happy. You always make me happy, Casey."

But on the flight home, she thought about it some more. "Missy, is it really that bad in Atlanta?"

"What do you mean, hon?"

"Tyler says he 'really, really, really' wants me there for the game on Thursday. Something about the crowd wanting to scalp him."

Missy frowned. "That doesn't sound like Tyler."

"I know, being bothered by a hostile crowd?"

Missy shrugged. "Maybe that's just his excuse and really, it's that he can't stand the thought of not seeing you for a whole week?"

"You think?"

Missy stuck the in-flight magazine back into the seat

pocket. "I think he's 'really, really, really' in love with you, is what I think. So yeah, that's a possibility."

Casey bit her lip. "If he's really in love with me, why hasn't he said so?"

"He hasn't?"

"Well, not in so many words. I mean, the other day he did say something like 'that's why I love you so much,' but it was sort of joking, you know? And when he was asking me to go to Atlanta, he said, 'there won't be anyone there to see me pitch who loves me.'"

Missy narrowed her eyes. "Hm. That is kind of...well...but Casey, do you love him? I mean, why haven't you said it to him if you do? Or are you waiting for him to say it first?"

Casey stared for a moment. "Um, I guess I am. I mean..."

"You *do* love him?" Missy asked. "It's totally okay if you don't, you know. I'm just trying to figure out where you're coming from."

Casey stuck her hands under her armpits like they were cold. "I think I do love him, but I'm not sure I believe it yet. I mean, it's still early, you know? And if he hasn't said it..."

"I don't know." Missy shook her head. "He might just assume you're in love. Both of you. You act totally like you are. You look like you are. So why would he think you aren't? And do you have to be in love with him to go to Atlanta?"

"Maybe?" Casey took out her day planner. "I would need to skip out on various things for work."

"So you're trying to figure out if you love Tyler more than you love your job?"

"I don't love my job, so I guess even if I only love Tyler a little, he wins."

"Well, there you go. Have fun in Atlanta."

That Thursday, Casey found herself rushing to the airport once again, and hopping on a flight to "the ATL." Tyler had impressively organized people to take care of her, so there was a driver waiting for her at the airport, and when she was dropped off at the ballpark, someone who worked for the team met her and escorted her up to a luxury suite. She thought that was a little odd, since how would Tyler even be able to tell she was there supporting him if she was up on the second level, behind glass? But she understood when only a few minutes later, Tyler himself sneaked through the door in full uniform.

"Oh my God, you're here." He wrapped his arms around her and just held her. "Thank you."

"You're welcome." She felt her own flood of relief at holding him—love or lust or whatever it was—not seeing him for five straight days had left her with a physical ache to be with him. There was maybe an hour still to go before game time, but out in the stands, the seats were filling up and music was blaring. The Robins were taking batting practice and she wondered if Tyler would be in trouble for skipping it, or if maybe since the ankle incident, he'd been banned from shagging flies. "So are you going to tell me..."

But she didn't get any further than that in asking him what was really so distressed about Atlanta, as he pulled her into a passionate kiss. Her blood began to heat up immediately and she succumbed to it for a while before pushing him back. "You tease," she said, voice hoarse. "I have to go straight from here to a plane back, you know."

"I know, but I just couldn't help myself," he said. Then he glanced at the clock and back at her. "Although..."

Vertigo swept through her. "Are you thinking what I'm thinking?"

"That I could just hitch you right up onto the counter in the private bathroom here?" he asked as he walked her backwards into the room, "and fuck you right here?" He lifted her up, pushing her summery dress back, and pulling her hips against his own at the edge of the counter. "Bet I won't even have to take your underwear off..."

She could feel his erection pressing against her and her own wetness welling up. "But you should," she said, "or they'll get all come-stained."

"All right." He held her in place with his hands on her hips, but nuzzled at her stomach until he had caught the edge of her waistband with his teeth. He lowered her panties carefully until they were hooked around one of her ankles. "There we go." He spread her legs gently, caressing up the insides of her thighs while she reached for the belt on his uniform.

The uniform not only had a belt, it had multiple layers of pants, something kind of like long johns on under there, plus other things, but eventually with his help, she freed his cock. He slicked it with her juices, which were flowing freely, and slipped into her with a gasp. "God, Casey, this..."

"Yeah," she said. She just seemed to want him more and more, which had a miraculous feel to her. She'd certainly never wanted someone so much she encouraged them to fuck her in a restroom. "God, you feel huge like this."

"Is it okay?"

"Yes. More than okay," she said. She squeezed him with

her interior muscles. "Now, no dawdling. You've got a game to pitch."

"Yes, ma'am." He started moving in her, keeping his hands wrapped around her ass. She slipped a hand between them to touch her own clit, and it wasn't long before she was coming. She came a second time quickly thereafter, and Tyler pumped her full of his come a few seconds later. *Yes, this no-condom business was certainly handy*, she thought.

He hurried out and she stayed in the restroom for a bit to clean herself up. When she emerged, her face was still quite flushed, but she was clean and her dress looked like she'd flown in it, but otherwise wasn't discernibly mussed.

At about twenty minutes before game time, a caterer came in and told her there wasn't any food ordered for her box, but she was welcome to use the bar and restaurant on the luxury level if she wanted anything to eat. She ended up sitting at the bar where she could see the field perfectly well, and having dinner there during the game. Tyler pitched six innings and left with a six-run lead. She decided she should get back to the airport and beat the traffic. The driver Tyler had hired was waiting, just a cell phone call away, and she was on a plane back to Boston by ten, getting onto an even earlier flight than she'd originally been booked for. She was in bed by two, which meant she got a short but decent night's sleep, and as it was, her boss sent them all home at two o'clock the next afternoon on Friday for "summer hours"—although it was actually that the computer network was down so they couldn't get that much done anyway. She had an afternoon nap and then loaded ESPN.com while she was reading her personal e-mail at home and looking at flights to Chicago for the road trip there, knowing Kim would kill her if she missed that one. A tiny video window in the corner of her screen started to play a Sportscenter broadcast.

She leaned closer as Tyler's name was being mentioned, hitting the key to turn up the volume.

"The Robins' Tyler Hammond has pitched himself into consideration for a slot in the All-Star Game, and maybe even the Cy Young Award, with the win he picked up in Atlanta last night," said a fresh-faced young anchorman. "It is his eighth straight win, and more importantly, he seems to be pitching better and better."

Tyler's face appeared, standing in front of what looked like a closet with his uniforms hanging in it. "Yeah, well, it was good that I got lucky, you know? That first one when I got ejected, the bullpen really held on, and there were a couple of other squeakers, but now the offense is clicking, Campbell is fitting right in, and you know, that gives me more confidence. So I pitch better, and the team does better...it's all coming together. You know?"

Casey chuckled. He didn't sound any different talking to a TV camera than he had to her dad the other night. She couldn't wait to talk to him on the phone that night and tell him she'd seen his interview. Even better, she couldn't wait for him to get home. His next start was on Tuesday, and Monday was an off day, so they'd get to have dinner and an evening together with no ballgame. And the team was in town for two weeks until the All-Star Break, so she'd get to see plenty of him for the next little while.

It was a lovely two weeks, and the good thing about three straight starts at home was that Casey got to meet a lot of the other wives—and they were all wives, no girlfriends, which she thought odd—and get recipes from nearly all of them. With Missy's help, soon she was getting a few e-mails per day with pieces for the cookbook, even one from Nakamura's wife with some traditional Japanese dishes. Mitsuko had sent a whole story with it about her husband being superstitious about what he ate before a big game, and the next thing she knew, Casey was e-mailing back to a bunch of the other wives asking for similar personal stories, and it just kept growing and growing. She ended up coming to the ballpark on some days when Tyler didn't even pitch.

She found herself working on the cookbook a lot while at work, which was fine, since it looked like she was working on a legitimate project. All of a sudden, going to work was more fun than it had been in a while. The finished cook book went off to the printer just before the home stand was over.

"So are you going to St. Pete for the All-Star Game?" Missy asked Casey one night at the ballpark as they headed up to the press dining room for some popcorn during a rain delay.

"Not as far as I know," Casey answered. "Tyler said he was picked, but because of the wonky ankle, he might not play. So he doesn't need me there."

Missy made a face, wrinkling her nose and eyebrows. "The point wouldn't be for you to watch him pitch the one measly inning he might do if they let him, but to go for all the hoopla and fun."

Casey shrugged. "I think we've got enough hoopla as it is. But I really can't take the time off work since I'm supposed to go on that trip to Chicago right afterwards. My best friend from college is there now and she's been after me to come visit."

"Oh, good. I'll try to come on that trip, too. Unless John's sick of me by then, since we'll have just spent three straight days together during the All-Star Break." Missy led the way to the door. "Travis!" She hugged him like she hadn't seen him in a long time.

"Missus Missy Madison," he said back. "And Casey Hammond."

"Er, Branigan," Casey said. "Don't get ahead of me now, Trav."

"Oh, my. Well, I'm sorry, my mistake," he stammered with a smile. "You know, we all just know you as Tyler's girl now. You ladies go on in."

Casey felt her cheeks flush, but she smiled back. When they had settled down with some popcorn, she wondered if she should ask Missy more about Tyler. Neither of them had used the word "love" again since the trip to Philly, and Casey was content with that, though she couldn't help but feel like maybe she ought to say something.

Instead she turned the question to Missy. "Is it my imagination, or are all the other 'wives and girlfriends' actually all wives?"

"Not your imagination," Missy said. "Not only do most ballplayers marry young, but most of the women chasing them are chasing that ring. Well, and even if they aren't, you know, each wants to be married to prove she isn't just a fling. Plus, you know, if you're away from your girlfriend half the year traveling...it's just different if you're married. Guys need to feel like what they've got waiting for them at home is really solid. And yeah, sure there are divorces and there's cheating and all that, but...that doesn't stop everyone from trying."

Casey nodded. "Makes sense."

"Ooh, here comes Ken. I want to pump him for information about this kid they're supposedly calling up from the minors to take Polanco's place."

"Which one's Polanco?"

"The backup catcher. The guy who catches on the days Doggy doesn't. There's rumors he's on the skids and this kid could come up. The kid could end up taking the starting job if he's good enough, though, so, you can see why I want to know." Missy stood and made a beeline for the writer fixing himself a cup of coffee.

Casey wasn't much interested in that conversation; she knew Missy would fill her in on anything important later, anyway. She picked up the sports section that was lying there from that day just to see if there was anything interesting about the Robins in it. There was a lot about the All-Star Game, and yes, here was a little story, just a few column inches, about Tyler and Campbell being the only two Robins going to the game.

Robins' management has asked All-Star team manager Tony LaRussa to keep Hammond out of the game because of his recently tweaked ankle. Said LaRussa to reporters yesterday, "I wouldn't want to mess with a guy's eleven-game win streak or his health. I'm honored to have Tyler Hammond on my staff, but no, we won't pitch him if the trainers want him to rest that ankle."

According to the Elias Sports Bureau, Hammond's eleven-game win streak is more impressive even than it looks, and it looks pretty impressive. Normally a pitcher being credited with an eleven-game win streak would include some no-decisions.

THE HOT STREAK

For Hammond to have actually earned eleven consecutive wins without any no-decisions is rare. The fact that he has been pitching deep into games, as well as the fact that the Robins bullpen has been strong, has helped his cause tremendously.

Casey noticed the byline on the story: Ken's. She got up and went to where Ken and Missy were standing by the coffee, waiting for a break in their conversation.

They both looked up at her.

"What's a no-decision?" she asked.

"Oh, well," Ken said, "There are multiple pitchers in a game, right? For both teams. Only one of them can be said to be the 'winner' and one the 'loser.' So even if your team wins, only one pitcher is the winning pitcher and the rest of the guys on the team are given 'no-decision.'"

"Okay, that makes sense. I was just reading what you wrote about Tyler."

"Pretty neat, isn't it? I hope the guys at Elias can figure out who holds the record for most consecutive winning decisions. If he keeps this up, it seems likely Tyler's got a shot at it, though. The record for most wins without a loss within one season is nineteen, and that was with no-decisions mixed in. So without those? He has to be close."

"That's...pretty neat." Casey found herself grinning. "I'll have to e-mail my dad and brother about that. Ever since we had dinner in Philly, they are huge Tyler Hammond fans "

"I'll e-mail you, too, if I find out anything more," Ken said. "In case you don't see the paper. 'The Streak' could become quite a story."

CHAPTER EIGHT

The All-Star Game was always played on a Tuesday, Casey learned, and the All-Star Break was three full days, Monday through Wednesday, when no games in the Major League were played at all. Three days didn't seem like much of a vacation to her, but the way people in baseball talked about it, after playing almost every day since the first of April, three days off in a row in mid-Julywas a huge relief.

She took Friday off from work and flew to Chicago Thursday night, where Kim picked her up at the airport and took her out for a late night dinner and drinks.

"So, you're still seeing this ballplayer..." Kim said, as they got their cocktails and looked out over the skyline of the city.

"Yes. Are you sure you don't want to go to the game? I can probably still get you a ticket."

"No, no, I'll be bored. I'll meet up with you after, though, so I can meet him. What time?"

"Well, that's the thing about baseball, you never know when the games are going to end." Casey shrugged. You never knew how long a football game was going to last either, what with time outs and overtimes and such, but baseball in particular seemed like it could go on all night. "It's a day game, though, so at least we won't be dragging back to the hotel at midnight. Why don't I call you when the game ends? Then give us an hour, hour and a half."

Kim sipped her cosmopolitan. "That must be hell on making dinner reservations."

Casey laughed. "Not really. When you're on ESPN every night for some reason restaurants always find room for you. It's...maybe the best perk about dating a ballplayer. I know that sounds really shallow, but...there you go. My parents were more impressed with his ability to get us a table than with his fastball."

"And what do they think of you going out with a celebrity?"

Looking out the window instead of at her friend, Casey shrugged. "Who knows, really? My mom thought it was nice that I found someone I like better than my job, though. But she was like, 'do you think you'll still be going out at Christmas time? We want to go to Aruba. Should we plan for both of you?'"

Kim laughed. "Well? *Are* you still going to be going out at Christmas time? You realize this guy is already past his expiration date."

Casey blinked. "What?"

"Don't you remember after you broke up with that guy Brad? Brent? Whatever the hell his name was, we were talking and you said they never last more than two months. That right at two months, your interest in a guy seems to just evaporate, like they go past their expiration date. Well, it's been longer than that for you and Tyler Hammond, hasn't it?"

"Well..." Casey had forgotten about that. With Tyler, the time just seemed to be flying by. "You're right. Two months would have been like two weeks ago..." And Tyler hadn't expired. Not in the least. "He just seems really, really into me. And I'm really into him. I can't explain it any better than that."

"Do you have low expectations?"

"What do you mean?"

"I mean, a lot of these other guys, you were measuring them on a lot of points, like did they have a good job? Would they make a good husband? A good father? That kind of stuff," Kim said. "You don't really seem to be thinking about that with Tyler, so maybe you're letting him be himself?"

"Hmm, maybe." Casey set her empty glass down, feeling the alcohol go to her head a little. "I mean, I went into it not even thinking we were having a date that first time, and things just kind of took off from there...are you saying maybe I let things grow because I didn't weigh it down with expectations? And so it could thrive instead of die?"

Kim set her own glass down. "I think that's what *you're* saying, and that's what counts."

"Huh. Yeah, I guess so." Casey smiled. "So I guess...I guess I should start admitting I'm in love with him."

"To him, you mean?" Kim asked.

"To myself," Casey said, leaning back in her chair and letting the booze swirl around in her brain. "Have to admit it to myself first. Seems pretty obvious, though, doesn't it?"

Kim laughed. "I'll let you know what it looks like after dinner tomorrow, how's that? But right now I'd say yeah, you are in it, and you are in deep, girl."

THE HOT STREAK

꙳

Casey spent the night at Kim's, then checked into the hotel in the late morning, missing Tyler, who was already on his way to the ballpark with the team. She followed, taking the El train to the ballpark. Like in Boston, it was easy to tell where to get off, as the train car became more and more crowded with people wearing baseball jerseys and hats, and they all got off the train en masse. Casey followed them to the park, found the window for her ticket and made her way into the park.

Wrigley Field was old and very different from the gleaming new ballparks she was used to, like the ultra-modern Robins' field and the luxury boxes in Atlanta. Everyone told her Wrigley was historic, and she felt a bit like she was visiting the Liberty Bell or some other landmark.

Missy hadn't come on this trip, and Shayna had but wasn't at the ballpark today because, she had said, she wanted to do some shopping on the Magnificent Mile. So Casey found herself sitting with a couple of the wives she didn't know as well, though they were friendly enough.

It was still a thrill to see Tyler go out to the mound and do what he did best. She knew athletes didn't consider themselves at all similar to performing artists, but she couldn't help the comparison. Watching him pitch felt to her like watching a musician or a dancer perform. If she'd been dating Mikhail Baryshnikov, or the lead singer of some rock band, wouldn't she feel like this? She was still uncomfortable with the idea of groupies, but the fact remained that it took a special figure to inspire that kind of devotion.

And he's mine, all mine, she thought, laughing to herself. *And he knows just how very special that is.* He struck out a batter and she found herself clapping—quietly, since most of the hometown crowd was booing.

In the third inning, a man slipped into the empty chair to her left. He was slightly balding, wearing a yellow polo shirt, and carrying a clipboard, which seemed odd. Every now and then he would make a notation on it, but mostly his eyes were on the field.

Tyler struck out two more in the third and the man whistled. "Ham is dealing," he said, more or less to himself, but partly in Casey's direction.

"And the batters are coming up bust?" Casey asked.

He chuckled. "You might say that. I don't know if the term comes from blackjack or poker or just baseball. But yes, you get the idea. He's struck out five out of nine batters right now, which is a really good clip."

Casey nodded.

"And he hasn't given up a hit. If he goes through the lineup again like that, then we can get really excited."

"Oh?"

"Yes. Three innings of no-hit ball, that's good, but if you can get through the lineup twice and still give up no hits, then you have a real chance to get all the way through the game with none."

"That's rare?"

"Very rare. Throw a no-hitter and you're guaranteed your cleats or glove will end up in the Hall of Fame."

Casey wasn't quite sure what that meant, but the man's voice had a reverence about it that told the story. "You think Tyler has a chance to do that?"

"It's possible. The Cubs aren't a very strong-hitting lineup. They have a lot of young free swingers, so they chase a lot of bad pitches. Hammond is smarter than they are and will toy with them like a cat with a mouse."

"Huh."

"Of course, no matter how good he pitches, it doesn't matter if his team doesn't score for him. If it stays zero-zero, it's got to be tough on him. This park is so small, with the wind blowing like it is, it's very easy to make a mistake and give up a home run."

"Oh." Casey watched as the opposing pitcher took his warm-up throws before the bottom of the inning. "But the other pitcher has that problem, too, right?"

"Right, that's true." The man turned and looked at her. "I'm Mike Garvin, by the way. I take it you know Tyler Hammond?"

"Um, yeah." She shook his hand. "I'm his girlfriend. Casey Branigan. So I'm still learning the baseball stuff."

"Oh, not a fan?"

"I wasn't, anyway. We met at my job, not his. I work for a magazine in Boston," she explained. People never knew what she was talking about if she said she worked for a service bureau, so it was simpler to say she worked for a magazine.

"Oh, outstanding," Mike said, and he sounded sincere. "My daughter just graduated from art school and is doing an internship at a magazine. Hopefully it becomes a paying job soon, but I guess it's like the Major League. You have to work your way in."

"Yeah."

"Well, Casey, here comes your man again."

"So what are you writing down?"

He showed her the clipboard. "I'm a scout. I'm tracking not just Hammond but a couple of other players." He had a pre-printed page of notes on each of them and was adding to them in pencil. "Nowadays we pull the radar gun readings and such off the Internet, but nothing beats what you can observe with your own eyes. Right now, he looks pretty good. Best I've seen him pitch all year."

They continued chatting through the fifth inning, then Tyler made it through the sixth, still without giving up a hit. Mike whistled appreciatively as the last man swung weakly at a pitch in the dirt and went back to the dugout looking dejected. "Right now, no one in the dugout will talk to Hammond, you know."

"Why?"

"Afraid they'll jinx him. See, a no-hitter isn't just about the pitcher doing great. It takes some luck, and ballplayers are superstitious. None of them wants to be the man who breaks his mojo somehow. One of the big superstitions is that you can't use the words 'no-hitter' or 'perfect game.'"

Casey tried to imagine Tyler sitting in the dugout alone with no one talking to him. "He must be going nuts. So how come you're not superstitious?"

Mike grinned. "I'm not rooting for the Robins, you know."

Casey looked at him in surprise. "You! You weren't going to tell me, were you?"

"Well, I figure why upset my nice neighbor?" He shrugged. "But I'll tell you something, if it looks like your guy there is going to do it, everyone in this crowd, even though they root for the other team, will get behind him and cheer because they want to see something rare and special. Everyone wants to see a historic event if they can."

He was right. Tyler got through the seventh without giving up a hit and Casey could feel the energy in the crowd. The next time he took the mound, there were some cheers for him, and as the first batter of the eighth inning went down on strikes, there was a fairly large roar from the crowd. Casey got goose bumps.

After the second man hit a fly ball caught at the wall, she said to Mike, "Do you think he can do it?"

"I know he has the ability to do it. The question is, *will* he do it?" Mike looked down at his clipboard. "The problem with all those strikeouts he throws is that he is already over one hundred pitches in the game. He's probably starting to get tired."

Now that Casey looked at Tyler, he did look tired. His shoulders were a little slumped, and she saw Mad Dog was out at the mound talking to him. "Doggy is giving him a rest by going out and talking to him," she said. That much she knew from things Missy had said before.

"Yes. And calming him down after the previous batter almost hit a homer, which could have not only broken up the no-hit bid, but lost them the game since there is still no score. Madison's a good catcher and they work together well."

Casey agreed. The final batter of the inning went down on a weak swing that hit the ball right to the first baseman, and a large cheer went up. "Wow."

"Yeah, wow is right, but the Robins still need to score to get anywhere."

Casey looked at the scoreboard. "Campbell's coming up. He'll hit a home run," she said confidently.

"You think so?"

"Yeah. He hasn't hit one in a while, and you said the ball was blowing out, and look how much bigger he is that the guy who almost hit one last inning." Casey knew there were a lot of other things that had to be taken into account, like how the Cubs pitcher threw, but she thought it was fun to try to predict.

Mike Garvin burst out laughing when on the very first pitch, Campbell did exactly that. The ball flew so far it went out onto the street.

Casey screamed and clapped her hands as he circled the bases. "That's the way, you big palooka!" Then she looked at Mike. "See, I told you so."

He laughed again. "I've been a scout for fifteen years, but I have to hand it to you. You called it."

That was the only run the Robins managed, but now if only Tyler could get three more outs, it would be history. Casey found herself holding her breath as he threw his warm-up pitches before the bottom of the ninth. "God, that sounds so dramatic, 'bottom of the ninth,' doesn't it?" she said to Mike. "Now I know why."

He just nodded, watching every move Tyler made.

Casey caught one of the other wives, Lila Gutierrez, looking back at her. When she saw her looking, Lila crossed herself and put her hands together like she was praying. Casey crossed her fingers.

The first batter went down swinging and the crowd erupted, getting to their feet. Casey and Mike stood, too, and Casey found herself fidgeting from foot to foot.

The second batter fouled off pitch after pitch and she could see on each one, Tyler looked more and more tired. But he wasn't going to give in. The batter swung again, this time hitting the ball high in the air. Mad Dog threw his mask off and caught the ball right by the dugout, and another huge cheer came out of the crowd.

"One more out, just one more out!" Mike said, incredulous.

"One more," Casey echoed in a whisper.

The final batter was a big guy who waved his bat menacingly as he stood at the plate. Everyone in the ballpark seemed to be holding their breath now, wondering if they were really, truly going to see something special.

Casey jumped as the sound of the ball hitting the bat cracked loudly and then the entire crowd groaned, followed by some cheers, as the ball landed cleanly in center field, a hit.

"Aw, damn it," Mike said. "One out away!"

Casey's eyes were on Tyler, visibly deflated, on the mound. Mad Dog and the whole infield had gathered around him and it looked like they were consoling him. Even the manager was there now. The manager patted him on the back and waved to the bullpen for a new pitcher. Tyler walked toward the dugout and seemed to realize people were giving him a standing ovation. He took his hat off and waved to the crowd, then going down into the dugout.

Casey sat back down. "Oh well. I guess it's time to start thinking about dinner."

Mike laughed. "Yeah. Although I hope your reservation's late. After a game like that, he's going to have to give a lot of interviews."

"Even though he didn't do it?"

"It's still a good story," Mike said. "Well, now that he's done, I'm done, too. Nice to meet you, Casey. It was great being neighbors."

She smiled and shook his hand. Out on the mound, Rigney, the closer for the Robins, was almost done warming up. Two pitches later, the game was done, and Casey found herself walking out with Lila Gutierrez, who seemed even more disappointed than Casey was.

"Bad break there, Casita," she said. "But he won. So his win streak is twelve now, yes?"

"Yeah, that makes twelve," Casey said. "I'm going to go back to the hotel and see if I can catch him on ESPN."

"You want to see if we can talk our way into the locker room? Well, they won't let us inside, but we can usually get to the door right by to wait for them."

"Nah, that's all right. I'll head back and just catch it in the bar there." *Let Tyler have his spotlight and take his time*, she thought. She didn't want him to rush through it because he thought she was hanging around waiting for him.

It took quite some time to get back to the hotel, thanks to the large crowd, but it was fun listening to everyone talking about Tyler. Tyler Tyler Tyler. She smiled inwardly. She couldn't wait to see him. It had been almost a whole week since they'd seen each other thanks to the All-Star Game and the travel to Chicago.

Once she got to the hotel, she called Kim to say Tyler might be a while yet, and then texted him to say she was in the bar. They had a widescreen TV still tuned to sports coverage, and she nursed a club soda with lime while waiting to see the report.

She didn't have to wait long for the familiar scene of Tyler standing in front of his locker with cameras and microphones all around him. Giant ice packs were bandaged to Tyler's shoulder, and he was shirtless, his hair wet and sticking up as if he'd taken a quick shower before meeting the press, but couldn't get dressed because of the ice.

THE HOT STREAK

"So what was going through your mind in the ninth inning?" asked a voice.

"Well," Tyler said, "I was mostly thinking, 'Thank God Campbell hit that dinger,' because now I actually had a shot at something. The no-hitter wouldn't mean much if we didn't win the game, you know? If I pitched nine no-hit innings and then we had to go to the bullpen at nothing-nothing? That would have been awful. No, I'd much rather that I won the game, that the team won the game, than I got the no-hitter. Although, man, it would have been nice, wouldn't it?"

The reporters laughed. "It's the second time you got that close, isn't it?"

"Oh yeah, in my rookie year, only my third start, I also got to ninth inning, two outs, and even two strikes! And then, God, I still see that ball flying into the stands in my nightmares. I hate Jack Villard forever for that one. No offense, Jack. If you're watching, you know I'm kidding, right?"

The reporters all laughed again.

Then a voice that sounded like Ken's asked, "So, that makes a streak of twelve wins in a row. Any comment about that?"

"Okay, you guys, I have something to tell you about The Streak. You remember the night it started? It was in Boston, and I had lost five in a row before that, right? And everyone was like, what's wrong with Tyler, right? You might remember I got ejected from that game and also fined for leaving early and all that." He paused while the reporters all laughed. "What I never told you guys was that I left early to go meet a girl."

Now there were more laughs. Casey found she couldn't move her hands from the top of the bar.

"No, seriously," Tyler went on. "I went to meet this girl, who I had met that day, just by chance, you know? But it was love at first sight."

Now there were only one or two laughs, as Tyler's face was earnest and serious. "I mean the kind you'd do anything to be with that person, the kind that just grabs you by the balls. Kind of love at first sight, okay? So, she was at that game, and I've been seeing her ever since. She's been at every game, and I seriously think she's my good luck charm. The Streak is all about Casey, and honey, if you're listening"—he turned and looked into the camera, then one of the others—"I love you, and please, please, please come to my start in Cincinnati next week?"

Casey just stared. "Oh my God."

The bartender eyed her. "You know the team is staying here, right?"

She laughed. "Yes, I know the team's staying here."

"Plenty of other guys, even if that one's taken," he consoled her.

Now she laughed harder. He thought she was a baseball Annie and had no clue he was talking about her. "Oh my God, yes, that one's taken."

A few minutes later, some of the guys and their wives came in, but there was no sign of Tyler. "He's on the late bus," Mad Dog said, when he saw her sitting there. "Still doing interviews."

"Did you...did you hear what he said?" Casey asked, barely able to keep from squealing. She was a little bit angry inside that he'd been keeping all this from her, but—but it was hard not to squeal when he'd just declared his love, undeniably. On national TV.

Madison grinned at her. "Did you doubt it, girl? He's crazy for you."

She just grinned back, and Mad Dog wandered away.

The next person she saw, though, was Ken. He came over to her and ordered a Coke as he climbed onto the stool next to hers. "Boy, what a day, huh? He nearly had that no-hitter in the bag."

"I know," Casey said, still grinning like a mad fool. "Wow, you got here quick."

"Hmm?"

"I could have sworn I just saw you on ESPN. Or heard you, anyway."

Ken chuckled. "That was taped earlier. I didn't stick around the park. Since I'm only doing a column, I didn't have to stay and file like the other writers." He turned and looked at her. "I have a question I want to ask you, Casey, but it's really kind of personal. And it isn't for a story or anything, so I...you..." He shrugged helplessly. "It's really none of my business. I should just shut up."

Casey looked back at him curiously. What could he want to know? What Tyler was like in bed? Couldn't be that. "You can always ask, Ken," she said. "I can always refuse to answer if it's something too personal."

He sipped his Coke through the cocktail straw. "That's true. Okay, here's the question, and if you don't want to answer it, you can just pretend I never said anything, okay? But here goes. How do you deal with Tyler's wife?"

Casey blinked and shook her head slightly as if she must have misheard him. "What?"

"Oh shit," Ken said, going white, his own mouth dropping open like hers. His reaction convinced her she'd heard it right.

"Wife?" she repeated, needing to know for sure that was what he had said.

"Wife," he repeated softly. "Lives in Tampa. I'd kind of forgotten they were still married, but she was at one of the All-Star shindigs last week. I take it...you didn't know."

Casey just shook her head. She couldn't feel her fingers. Tyler had never, ever mentioned being married, not even being *formerly* married. And Missy! Missy had never mentioned anything about it either! "They're still married?"

Ken winced. "They're separated, I think, but not divorced. Oh God, I told you it was none of my business." He looked miserable.

But not nearly as miserable as Casey felt. "Oh my God, I'm like Jimmy's mistress, aren't I?"

"Oh no, I don't think it's like that..." Ken said quickly.

"Ken! You just said it was none of your business!" She couldn't help it. She snapped at him. "Oh shit, and I even took him to meet my parents and everything! God, I'm stupid. Stupid, stupid, stupid."

The next thing she knew, she was on her way up to the room, grabbing her suitcase, and then calling Kim on the phone. The tears didn't start to fall until she was in the taxicab on her way to Kim's. She could see the sympathetic eyes of the cabbie in the rear view mirror, but she'd be damned if she was going to explain why she was crying. It was almost too humiliating to think about, much less say out loud.

CHAPTER NINE

Thank God for Kim, who listened to her rants and crying and just kept plying her with tequila each time Casey thought of one more thing that hurt. "Oh, God, all that talk about how there was *me and only me*, and he's *married!*"

"Separated," Kim pointed out. She had taken to saying the word quietly every time Casey said the word "married," although it didn't seem to be having much of an effect.

"How could he not even mention her? I'm so dumb."

"Case, you're in love, and he's in love, and everyone does stupid things when..."

"God, all that talk about how there was 'no one who loved him' in Atlanta and he wanted me there, and all the time it was a stupid superstition? Oh God, I feel sick. We had sex in the bathroom before that game—was all that sex really about baseball and not me at all?" She put a hand over her mouth.

"Jeez, Case." Kim handed her a glass of water this time.

Casey's phone rang and she looked at the number. Tyler had already tried to call twice and she had sent it to voice mail both times, then saw that the coward didn't even leave a message. It was a Boston area code, but she didn't recognize the number. "Fuck it." She didn't answer and stuck the phone back in her pocket.

Kim sighed and went to refill her water glass. "You should probably be telling *him* all these things, not me, you know."

"What, and give him a chance to make up some other story and make a fool out of me all over again?" She saw her tequila glass still had some in it and she reached for it, draining it, then set it back down on the coffee table.

Kim put the water glass back in her hand and swept the others into the kitchen quickly. "You want me to call him? I'll give him an earful for you, and he can't fool me. I'm not in love with him."

"I'm not in love with him either!" Casey shouted, then burst into tears, because as she said it she felt a stabbing pain in her chest. It was patently not true. "Except that I am," she said through sobs.

"I know, hon, I know," Kim said, sitting back down next to her and hugging her. "If you didn't love him, it wouldn't hurt like this."

"Stupid fucking idiot," Casey said, without specifying whether she was talking about Tyler or herself.

Her phone rang again. This time when Casey dug it out of her pocket, Kim took it from her. "Casey's phone, Casey can't talk right now, can I help you?"

Casey heard the mumble of a male voice, but it didn't sound like Tyler. She was half wishing it was him, half dreading it.

"Well, you'll probably have to ask her about that, but like I said, she's in no shape to talk right now."

"Who is it?" Casey croaked, trying to stop crying.

"Somebody named Mad Dog."

Casey grabbed the phone out of Kim's hand. "Madison, you tell that no-good shit that the next girl he wants to declare eternal love to had better know about his goddamn wife and by the way ESPN is *not* a Valentine's service and he can take his fucking winning streak and *shove it up his ass!*"

A very small, tinny voice answered calmly. "You got it, Casey."

"Oh shit, Mad Dog, I didn't mean to scream at you, but..." But she burst into tears again.

"Um, no apology necessary," he said. "Hey, I'll let you go, but, Missy really wants to call you, too. Should I tell her to wait until tomorrow?"

"Yeah." Casey hung up and flung the phone aside. It disappeared into the couch.

Kim sighed. "Valentine service?"

"Tsk. Best I could come up with on short notice."

"If not for the whole wife thing, I thought his declaration of love on national television was actually kind of romantic."

Casey got shakily to her feet. "That's the problem. The entire thing, everything he's said to me has been romantic, until I look at it in light of what he hasn't been saying." She swore again. "Even all the 'I really can't wait to see you' stuff...he always, always, always engineered our dates to be the night before he pitched. How did I miss that? People even kept saying, hey, don't tire him out, don't stay out too late, all that kind of stuff. But I believed it. I believed he just really wanted me, needed me." She went unsteadily toward the bathroom. She was much drunker than she'd realized while sitting still. Walking was a bit of a challenge, but she made it to the door, then turned the water on and splashed her face.

Kim followed her, standing in the doorway and watching her in the mirror as Casey looked at her own reflection. Her eyes were completely red and puffy. "I look like something from a NyQuil ad," Casey said, miserable.

"I'm so sorry, Case."

Casey looked at her. "You look like you want to say something else."

Kim shook her head. "I'm sure there's more to the story. But I won't argue with the fact that he made a huge mistake here, and you're both paying for it."

Casey sat down on the lid of the toilet. "Oh, don't say that."

"What, that he's hurting, too? I'm sure he is, even if it's all his own damn fault."

"Stop it!" Casey growled, balling her fists. "It is his fault. Just let me be angry at him right now."

"Okay."

"Oh God, I think I'm going to be sick. I mean, really sick."

"I'll just leave you to that, then." Kim closed the door.

The next day, Casey woke to a skull-crushing hangover and three text messages, two from Tyler and one from Missy. She deleted the ones from Tyler and looked at the one from Missy while Kim brewed some coffee and made some plain toast. Missy was offering to pick her up at the airport and wanted to know when her flight was getting in. She texted back with the time, then lay her head on Kim's butcher block table. "This time yesterday, my life was perfect."

Kim set a mug down near her. "No, it wasn't. You were all

in a lather trying to figure out how much you loved him and how he felt about you. Well, now you know."

"Yeah, thanks, look on the bright side." She sat up and took the coffee but didn't drink it, just held the warm cup in her hands. "So, seriously, do you think I should give him a chance to defend himself?"

Kim brought over the toast and some blackberry jelly, and sat down across from her at the breakfast nook table. "Well, if you're planning to break up with him over this, it's really hard to just walk away and never see him again, you know? That only happens in, like, movies. Usually there's some messy post-processing."

"Ugh." Casey nibbled at the crust of her toast. "I guess real adults would at least talk about it, huh? I really want to just change my phone number and move and pretend we never met. Quit my job, too. How's that for an excuse, finally? Yeah, my ex-boyfriend turned into a stalker and so I'm moving to Seattle or something. Or Portland." Portland was better. No baseball team.

"I'm not saying you owe him a chance to defend himself or anything," Kim said carefully, "but for your own sake, you need to say some stuff to him. Not to me, but right to him, and you ought to do that to his face instead of in e-mail. It feels great to write that 'fuck you, Charlie' letter, but it's not the same." She spread jam on her own toast and then bit into it. "When do I have to get you to the airport?"

"Couple of hours. Ugh. My God. How much you want to bet half my office saw the declaration of love on ESPN? And they are going to be bugging me all day Monday about it and I'm going to have to t-tell them...that I..." She felt ill all over again.

"Hush, hon, one thing at a time. Let's not stress over stuff that hasn't even happened yet. Someone's picking you up at the other end, is that what you said?"

"Yeah. Missy Madison. I told you about her, the catcher's wife?"

Kim nodded. "She sounded like a nice person. I'm sure she'll have something good to say."

As it turned out, the first thing Missy said after Casey got into the car and she'd hugged her was, as if it were all one long word: "GoddamnthatstupidassTylerHammondanyway."

"Yeah," was all Casey could say as they pulled away from the curb.

They drove in silence for a few minutes while Missy merged into traffic exiting the airport. Missy spoke first. "Okay, so, what exactly happened? Because you know I got it only in bits and pieces from Doggy."

Casey took a deep breath before starting. "Did you see the game yesterday?"

"Yeah, I turned it on around the fifth when I heard it was a no-hitter." Missy chanced a look at her. "What does that have to do with it?"

"Well, just, it was such a big game, Tyler was staying extra late doing more interviews and things. And you know how...how high he gets."

Missy nodded.

"The bigger the game, the loopier he is after, right? Adrenaline or whatever. Anyway, so there he is, totally in love with the entire universe after a win like that, and he busts out on national television all about how it was love at first sight with me and how the winning streak has been ever since I've been going to his games."

152

"Yeah, I saw that, too."

Casey gritted her teeth. "So, okay, while watching that, I was totally with him, I was totally won over like it was this huge, huge thing he was doing for me, because he loved me, winning the games, or like my love somehow was what gave him the extra oomph to win, or something, right? But then I'm thinking to myself, wait a sec, if it's so damn important to him that I'm part of The Streak, then why didn't he ever say so to me before? He's never ever said anything to *me*. And that trip to Atlanta..." She broke off, her cheeks flushing.

"Oh, babe."

Casey forced herself to go on. "He totally talked me into skipping work and all that to meet him in Atlanta, to be there when he pitched, because he said he didn't want to pitch in front of the hostile crowd."

"That fucker. I remember you saying that and thinking what the hell was up with that."

"I mean, was he afraid I'd be like, 'your superstition is stupid, to hell with you?'"

Missy craned her neck, trying to see if there was anyone in the exit lane, then horned her way in between two SUVs. She was driving a small sports car and the driver behind her honked angrily.

"Yeah, yeah," she said to the driver, then to Casey, "Well, what do you think you would have said if he told you?"

"I don't know. But maybe if he'd told me he loved me sooner, the superstition wouldn't seem so stupid." She clutched her purse in her lap. "So then, on top of all that, I'm on the one hand just floating happy because of the I-love-you stuff on TV, even as I'm wondering what was up with not saying anything to me about The Streak—you know, like is it something like how you're not supposed to say 'no-hitter' during a no-hitter—in comes Ken, to the bar where I'm watching."

"Oh no."

"Oh yes. And he's like 'maybe this is personal, but...how do you feel about that, given that Tyler's married to another woman?'"

"Oh shit."

"Yeah."

Neither of them spoke as Missy navigated through the city streets toward Casey's apartment. Finally they had reached the building. "What a dumbass," Missy said as she threw the car into park and hit the flashers. "I could kill him right now."

"Me too," Casey said quietly.

"Look, do you want to be alone? Or do you want to grab some coffee or something?"

Casey looked up at her friend. "Did he put you up to talking to me?"

Missy pursed her lips. "He begged me like a dying man in the desert for a sip of water," she said. "But I was going to talk to you anyway. And he knows he's on my shit list for more than one reason."

"Oh?" Now Casey was curious.

"Yeah. John literally stayed up all night with him last night, pretty much talking him down off the ledge, although he didn't actually climb out the window. You know what I mean. And the result is that John's not playing today, and they are letting that hotshot kid catch, and I really am going to kill Tyler if his shenanigans end up losing my husband his job."

Casey put her hand over her mouth. "Holy crap."

"Yeah. So I'm not exactly feeling super charitable toward

Mr. Ham and Cheese right now. So if everyone's looking for someone to talk you into making up with him, I don't know if I'm it right now."

Casey pointed to a car pulling out up ahead. "Go park up there and come upstairs. I've got coffee and tea and I think there's half of a grocery store coffee cake I didn't finish."

A few minutes later, they were sitting on Casey's IKEA couch, with mugs of tea and the untouched cake sitting on a plate on the coffee table. "So should I have *asked* him about the whole wife thing?"

Missy sipped her tea. "How would you know to? And honestly, I thought for sure they finalized the divorce during the off season, *last* off season! But even John doesn't know why he didn't say goodbye to her legally yet, even though they've been separated for more than a whole year. My guess is she's been in no rush or wants more money or something."

Casey shivered. "Do you think they're getting back together?"

"Jeez, Casey, I don't know. I doubt it, though."

"What's her name? I don't even know her name."

"Linda. Linda Maroni, I think." Missy cut a tiny sliver of cake and shook her head slowly while eating it with her fingers. "What the hell was Tyler thinking? That you wouldn't find out? Or was he so wrapped up in you that he *forgot* about her?"

"Ugh, that's almost more horrible than he just didn't have the guts to tell me."

"Yeah, you're right."

They were quiet for a while, Casey trying to imagine what all went on in Tyler Hammond's head. Her phone started to ring. She began digging it out of the bottom of her purse. "Did he really cry about me all night?"

"He did. John doesn't make that kind of stuff up."

It was a number she didn't recognize. She showed it to Missy, whose eyes went wide. "That's the assistant GM of the team. You better answer it."

"Maybe it's about the cookbook?" Casey asked. It was due to be shipped directly to the ballpark some time this week. She should check on that, she thought as she flipped the phone open. "Hello?"

"Um, Miss Branigan?" asked a tentative male voice. "This is Gene Billingham, the Robins'..."

"I know who you are."

"Oh, okay, sure, just checking. Um, I know you've, um, well, had some angst recently..."

Casey laughed, short and bitter. "And?"

"And, well, I realize that this is a bit of an odd request, but...but we do take the mental and physical well being of our players very seriously. Mr. Hammond represents a multimillion dollar investment and, well, I'm sure you don't want to hear about that. But the Robins organization would like to know what it would take to convince you to come to Cincinnati in a few days." He sounded nervous as hell.

"They want me to go to Cincinnati," she said to Missy, then to Billingham, "What do you mean, 'what would it take' to convince me?"

"Well, we understand you and Mr. Hammond have had a falling out, but the team would very much like you to be there. Um, it may sound strange to you, but we take Hammond's win streak very seriously, and well, we'd really, really like you to be there. We'll arrange your flight, limo service, accommodations, everything, if you'll say yes."

Missy leaned close to hear what he was saying. She made a motion with her hand, rubbing her thumb across her fingertips. Casey raised her eyebrows as if to ask if she was serious. *Ask for money?* Missy nodded.

"Well, Mr. Billingham, I'm very busy. The service bureau I work for typically hires me out for off-site jobs for a hefty fee."

"How hefty?" The man was practically jumping at the chance that she might say yes. Casey was thinking it usually ran around five hundred dollars per day, around fifty dollars per hour, and she was considering asking for a thousand just to see what he'd say, when he blurted out, "Would five thousand dollars do it?"

Missy was shaking her head. "What if you lose your job over this?"

"Well, I don't know," Casey said to him carefully. "I've been taking a lot of time off because of baseball lately, and my boss isn't very happy about that. And she'll be really unhappy at an impromptu trip on such short notice..."

"Miss Branigan. We'd be happy to pick up the rest of your salary for the year if that's what it would take. Are we talking fifty thousand?"

"Yes," Casey said.

"Great!" His voice brightened considerably. "I'll pass you to my secretary to take your bank account information so that fifty thousand can be wired to you directly, and to get your address and so forth to set up your airport limousine."

"Wait... " Casey hadn't meant for them to pay her whole salary, just "the rest of the year." But apparently he'd misunderstood her. "Um...I meant, which day is it? That I'm going?"

"Wednesday," he said. "Please hold for my secretary."

The Hot Streak

Casey squeezed the phone while she was on hold and said to Missy, "Does everyone in baseball treat money like it's Monopoly money?"

"Pretty much," Missy said. "See if she'll book me on the same flight, too, if you want me to go along."

Casey nodded. "Yeah, I might need the moral support."

~

Casey realized how weak her geography was when she found out the Cincinnati airport was actually in Kentucky. "I had no idea Ohio bordered Kentucky," she said to Missy as they rode to the hotel. "I think I've always assumed Kentucky was further south."

Missy laughed. "Failure of the American education system. So we're at the Westin and they have a spa, and I thought I should let you know I took the liberty of booking a facial and a massage. For both of us, I mean. The team doesn't want you at the ballpark until like five thirty, six o'clock, so we have plenty of time for it."

Casey smiled a little sadly at her friend. "I don't know if it's a good idea."

"A massage?"

"I don't even know what a facial is, really. I've never had one."

Missy goggled at her. "You're kidding, right? You never did a spa day when being someone's bridesmaid or something?"

Casey shook her head.

"They basically massage your face and kind of steam-clean it. It feels really good and it's relaxing, and combine it with a body massage and you'll be completely relaxed by the time we go. Besides, I'm pretty sure I'm getting it billed to the team, too."

Now Casey laughed. "Monopoly money again? I still can't believe there's fifty grand in my bank account right now." Casey hadn't gone to work on Monday. She had e-mailed her boss saying just, "family emergency" and let them think what they wanted. There was no chance they hadn't seen that ESPN report, but she didn't care what they thought. She had bigger worries right now.

"Look, they'd happily spend fifty grand without blinking on a team psychologist, right? If flying you in and paying you to quit your job keeps Tyler from self-destructing, it's a bargain."

"I didn't actually quit the job. You think the team is going to want me to go to all his starts?"

"Unless he loses tonight, in which case, well, The Streak's broken." Missy shrugged.

Casey was surprised to find she didn't want that to happen. She still wanted to kill Tyler Hammond, but she didn't want him to lose. *He's crazy, baseball's crazy, and I'm crazy, too,* she thought.

The massage and facial were so relaxing that while the masseuse was working on her back, Casey fell asleep. The woman gently woke her to turn over a while later, and she promptly fell asleep again on her back. She hadn't been sleeping well at all, and she awoke feeling slightly refreshed. She also learned they could walk to the ballpark from the hotel.

THE HOT STREAK

Missy wanted to take a cab, but Casey convinced her to put on more sensible shoes and they walked down the hill to the park. Off to one side of the ballpark, a bridge that looked a lot like the Brooklyn Bridge spanned the river. The park itself was round and white with colored accents; from a distance it reminded Casey of a big cake.

Up close it was like most other ballparks. Missy got her ticket at the window and Casey was surprised to find she had not just a ticket but what looked like a backstage pass to wear on a string around her neck. "What am I supposed to do with this?"

Missy helped her put it on. "It says it gives you field, press box, and clubhouse access, which is unusual. Wives usually aren't allowed in the clubhouse. Why don't we go to our seats? My guess is Tyler pulled some strings to get it for you, hoping you'll come down and talk to him."

"As if." Casey had deleted several more text messages from him without reading them, as well as some voice mails. She knew *he* knew she was doing that, as the message went back to him via the Madisons.

They made their way to their seats, which were right beside the dugout. The Robins were on the field taking batting practice. As in Atlanta, it didn't look like Tyler was out there. They hadn't been sitting there for ten minutes when a reporter recognized Casey and came hurrying over. "Um, Miss Branigan, could we interview you about Tyler Hammond?"

Casey and Missy exchanged a look.

The reporter was a fresh-faced kid, probably younger than Tyler, in a very expensive suit that gave him the look of someone who wore clothes his mother picked out. "I know it's kind of personal, but people are loving the love-at-first-sight angle, you know? So we were thinking if we had a few segments from you, we could play them during the game if he pitched well. You know?"

Missy leaned over and whispered in Casey's ear. "The press doesn't know you're on the outs."

"Shit," Casey said under her breath. She smiled up at the kid. "Um, I don't know. What kind of thing would it be?"

"Oh, er, well, here, these are the questions I have for you." He pulled a notepad from an inside pocket of his jacket and flipped one page, then showed it to her. The questions read:

How did you meet?

Was it love at first sight for you, too?

Do you think love can really make a difference in a game like baseball?

How does it feel to be part of a potentially history-making accomplishment? Your name in the baseball history books with his?

Casey handed the notebook back to the kid. Just thinking about her potential answers had misted her eyes and she tried to speak calmly. "I...I really can't. Maybe...maybe if he wins tonight, though, okay?"

"Okay. Thanks for considering it." He hurried away.

Missy exchanged a look with her. "If he wins tonight?"

"I'm going down there to give him a piece of my mind," Casey said, standing up. "The rat bastard. Does he think I'm just going to sit here and be on all the cameras and everything and that will make it okay?"

Missy waved to someone on the field frantically. Casey wasn't pleased to see it was Ken. "Come here, come here! Ken, can you take Missy down to the clubhouse?"

THE HOT STREAK

"I don't actually want to go in there," she said. "But I want to talk to him."

"Well, I..." Ken stammered.

"You owe her," Missy growled.

Ken sighed. "Yeah, I do. Come on." He held his hand up so Casey could take it and climb over the short wall onto the field. "I'll take you up the tunnel from the dugout to there."

The dugout was empty except for a bat boy who didn't pay them any attention. All the Robins players were on the field taking batting practice or shagging fly balls. Ken and Casey made their way up a narrow concrete hallway to a wider concourse. Across that hall was a heavy metal door marked "Visitors."

"Stay here," Ken said. "He's in the bullpen warming up right now, I'm sure. I'll go around to there and tell him you're here."

Casey found herself standing there for what felt like quite a while. Various employees and other traffic made their way past her, including some large golf carts moving kegs of beer and other supplies, but no one paid her any attention. At one point a gray-haired man in a security guard's uniform came by and blinked at her, but after a glance at the tag around her neck, he meandered on.

The door burst open with a loud bang as it hit the wall and Tyler flew into her arms. Well, more accurately, he flew at her and she put her arms up in defense and ended up in a bear hug. "Oh God, you're here, you're here. Thank you. Oh my God, thank you."

She pushed at him until finally she pinched him hard in the ribs through the many layers of his uniform and he jumped back with a yelp. "Tyler! You asshole! Keep your fucking hands off me!" He smelled like grass and sweat and laundry detergent.

He stared wide-eyed for a second. "Okay." He looked like he really didn't know what to do with his hands, then, and he jammed them into his back pockets. "Sorry. I was just...I couldn't help it. I've been dying to see you."

"I bet."

"No really, Case." Now he was looking at the concrete floor between them, head hanging. "I just...I know I fucked up, big time."

"This isn't like grade school, Tyler, where you can just promise to try harder next time and everything's okay." She crossed her arms.

"Okay, I know that, I do. But I have to start somewhere. I figure an apology is a good place for that." He suddenly looked up as the sound of something crunching reached their ears. "Oh shit, here comes the team. Look, I have to go back in there, but I'll be back. I'll come talk to you in the top of the first, okay? While we're batting I'll have time. I just have to ask you to promise me one thing."

"What?" She turned and looked down the tunnel and sure enough, the players' cleats crunched against the fake grass-style carpet, getting closer.

"I need you to be totally, completely honest with me, okay?"

"You need *me...?*" She stared incredulous. "Tyler, you're the one who hid things, who..."

"I know. I know. Total disclosure from me, too, okay? Both of us, the whole story, the true story, we don't hold anything back, okay?"

"Okay, but..." But the rest of the team had reached them

and Tyler let himself be carried by the tide back into the club-house. Mad Dog saw her standing there and gave her a grim nod of acknowledgement.

Then she was standing alone at the top of the tunnel again. A few minutes later, Mad Dog came back out and handed her a cold, unopened bottle of water.

"Thanks."

"Don't mention it." That was all he said before he disap-peared back into the locker room.

Casey found herself pacing up and down the corridor some. In a little nook off to one side, she eventually found a white bucket that had only a few dirty, worn-out baseballs in it. She dumped them out and carried the bucket back to the spot by the door, turned it upside down and sat on it. She cracked open the water and took a sip. The summer heat of Cincinnati that had not seemed like much on the breezy walk to the ballpark as the sun set now seemed to be seeping into her as she sat there.

There was a clatter as the team emerged again, heading down to the dugout. As Tyler passed her, he said "National An-them!" and gave her a thumbs-up.

About five minutes later, he came hurrying back up the tun-nel. "Okay, sorry about that. We get fined if we miss the an-them."

She stood and crossed her arms. "You sure it isn't just that you're superstitious that if you miss the anthem, you might lose? You've heard it before every game you've won, after all."

He shook his head. "How about that promise? I promise. Casey, I'll answer any question you have. I'll tell you everything I'm thinking. All of it, the truth, completely." His eyes were wide and he looked like he wanted to chew his lip and was only stopping himself by sheer force of will.

"All right, I promise." She lifted her hand like she was taking the Boy Scout pledge, but she was serious. "So? You were trying to apologize and doing a crap job of it."

He leaned against the wall like he didn't have the strength to hold himself up. "Yeah. Okay. I was wrong not to tell you about Linda. We are trying to get divorced. Truthfully. We did most of the paperwork, or, our lawyers did, but there's a last few things we both need to sign, and well, you probably know by now, we never signed them. Um, I was supposed to sign them when we were in Tampa during spring training and I didn't."

"Why?"

"I—I don't know. I just couldn't. I gave her the house, all that stuff, but I just couldn't put my name on that paper without talking to her one last time, you know. She wasn't there. Her lawyer brought me the papers. Her lawyer looked like he was going to kill me. But then she didn't call me to bitch me out. Linda, I mean. So I started to wonder if maybe it was a reprieve. Maybe she had second thoughts after all. Maybe we had a chance, and a break from each other was all we needed. I e-mailed her to say, you know, she was there when we tied the knot, so I really wanted her there when we untied it."

Casey gritted her teeth. "Are you telling me you're still in love with her?"

"I'm getting to that! One thing at a time. No, no, I'm not in love with her, but at the time I didn't know that." His head jerked up as a sharp whistle came echoing up the tunnel.

THE HOT STREAK

"Damn it. That's the bat boy telling me I have to get my ass down there to pitch. You'll stay here, right? I'll come back up next inning, okay?"

She sat back down on the bucket. "Okay." She tried to imagine Tyler arguing with Linda. *It's not just a piece of paper. It's our real marriage,* he'd say. She could imagine it in his voice. Was Linda one of those "real" women he always said he prized, or was she the supermodel type? Casey had no idea.

From here, she also couldn't tell what was happening in the game. She could hear the bursts of music, some applause. If Tyler was pitching, applause was probably bad since they weren't at home. *Oh, who the hell cares how the game is going?* But after all those months of hanging on every pitch, she found she couldn't just ignore it.

She texted Missy. *What's happening out there?*

A text came back almost immediately. *Where are you?*

Right outside the clubhouse in the tunnel. Tyler says he'll talk to me while the Robins are batting.

What did he say so far?

Nothing much. Divorce never finalized because Linda sent her lawyer and he wanted her to come face to face. So what's happening in the game?

Tyler has struck out one, then walked a guy, oh look, double play. One more out and then he'll be on the way to you.

Casey sighed. About five minutes later, Tyler came back up the tunnel, out of breath and sweating. "Okay, so where were we?"

"You weren't in love with her but you didn't know that," Casey said, standing up.

"Right." He took a deep breath and then went on. "Yeah,

166

so, I haven't been in love with her for a while, but...that didn't mean I wasn't trying to be optimistic and hope that things could still work out, you know?"

"Just like you're doing now?" she demanded.

He blinked. "Yeah, I guess. I mean, if I didn't think there was some chance to work it out between you and me...should I even bother, Casey? Do you love me?"

Now it was Casey's turn to blink. She'd just made a promise to be completely honest. That meant with herself and with him. "Yeah, Tyler, I love you. The question is if I can keep loving you when you've broken it all so badly."

He nodded. "That's fair. For what it's worth, Case, I meant every word I said on TV. I fell for you really hard right away. I mean, *hard*. I could barely believe it when you agreed to go to that game, and then me skipping out on the team early? I know they all say I do crazy things, but I'd never done something like that."

"How big was the fine?" Casey asked suddenly. "You told me before you were fined, but you didn't say how much."

"Oh, um. I think it was ten thousand dollars. Because they were really, really pissed at me and it wasn't my first offense. The fine goes in the form of a donation to the team charitable foundation, so it's not like it really matters. But, yeah."

Casey just shook her head, thinking *Monopoly money.* But still. He'd essentially paid ten grand to take her on a date.

"Anyway, I really fell hard for you, and just...well, you know how things went that night."

"You didn't even tell me the truth that night," she said. "That you lived at the Ritz. That you ate there almost every night. You said 'oh, I come here a lot.'"

He had the good grace to look guilty at that. "I just...didn't want you to think I was pathetic and lame. Ah, shit." There was the whistle again. "Back in a few."

He jogged back down the tunnel and Casey finished off the bottle of water.

He'd given her a lot to think about and now she had ten to fifteen minutes to wait for him to come back. If he was telling the truth, if he really was keeping to his promise and telling her everything, then he really was as good as divorced from his wife, wasn't he? Could she really blame him for not having signed the final papers yet?

But was she in love with the real Tyler, or the Tyler who tried to put on a good image for her, who didn't tell her about where he lived because he was afraid of what she might think? Didn't she know him better than that, though?

She texted Missy. *Is it stupid that the person I want most to comfort me when my heart hurts is Tyler himself?*

The answer came back. *Not stupid at all. Three outs, here he comes.*

Tyler leaned against the cinderblock wall next to her. "Okay. I'm sorry about that, too. The Ritz thing, I mean. There really isn't much else I hid, though, Case. You got to know me really fast."

She shook her head. "What about the whole fact that you had a winning streak going?"

His face fell. "Um, yeah, that was the other big thing. But I couldn't tell you about it."

She crossed her arms again. "Because of superstition? Like with a no-hitter?"

"No, because it would have meant telling you how in love with you I was." He shook his head, as if he hardly believed how stupid he'd been. "And I didn't want to do that and scare you off. Because I thought, *this girl, maybe she just wants a summer fling with a ballplayer*, you know? I just wasn't sure. You didn't...you never said anything really...commitment-y."

Casey's jaw dropped. "What did you call all that about...about...about sex without a condom and being exclusive with each other?"

He stared at her. "You never said it was because you loved me. You seemed to think it was really hot, but you never said anything to me. I got...I had the feeling you were still trying to figure out how you felt about me. Even when we met up with your parents. It really seemed to me like you were not really sure. Am I totally off base?"

"Yes." But Casey bit her lip. *Total honesty, remember*. She was starting to realize why he'd made her promise it, too. "Well, no. You're not off base. I was...kind of trying to figure it out for myself at the time."

The damn whistle jarred her out of her train of thought, though. He touched her lightly on the shoulder before running back down the tunnel.

Casey kicked the clubhouse door as soon as he was out of sight. Was it her fault? Because *she* hadn't been able to tell how she felt, *he'd* held back how he felt?

No. No, this is not *my fault*. She banged her fist on the door, and then was surprised when it opened. "Can I help you?" A short man in a polo shirt with the Robins logo on it was standing here.

She was red-faced and stammered. "Oh, n-no. Sorry. That was an accident. But um, you don't happen to have more bottled water in there?" She held up her empty bottle. This arguing stuff was thirsty work.

THE HOT STREAK

"I can refill it if you want," he said. "Water or Gatorade?"

"Just water, thank you." She handed him the bottle, and he shut the door in her face.

A minute later, he reappeared. "Here you go, miss."

She sipped it gratefully as she sat on the bucket. Then she texted Missy. *Is it my fault if I didn't know how I felt, whereas he actively hid how he felt?*

Of course not, came the answer. *How were you supposed to figure out how you felt if he was hiding from you?*

That seemed to make a lot of sense, so when Tyler came back during the top of the fourth inning, that was what she told him. "Don't you dare blame *me* for this mess. I couldn't tell you how I felt because I was trying to figure it out, and how did you expect me to figure it out if you were hiding your part of the relationship from me? No wonder I was so confused."

"But if I'd known you wouldn't run away, I would have told you sooner," he said plaintively.

"So what was I supposed to say? 'I promise I won't run away if, by the way, you might be hiding something from me?' Tyler, that doesn't make any sense."

"Um, I guess not. But it's still true. I wanted to tell you. But I was afraid." He slid down the wall and sat on the concrete floor. He looked tired and worn, and his uniform was sweaty. "I wanted to tell you about how I felt, and I figured The Streak wasn't probably going to keep going, though, you know? I figured I'd lose a game, or the bullpen would blow one at least, and then I could at least forget about that part of it, and just deal with the normal relationship issues, you know?"

She stayed on the bucket. "Did you fly me to Atlanta just to have sex with me?"

He looked up at her. "Are you asking if I was afraid The Streak would break if we didn't fuck? Or are you asking if the thought of going ten days without you, without seeing you or touching you, didn't feel like it was going to be like going without water or food all that time?"

"Both."

He slumped and answered. "Both."

She was silent for a bit. "You didn't think I'd feel used?"

He slumped even further and his voice was very small. "I figured if you loved me, you'd understand how important it was. And if you didn't, well, maybe it was just a big adventure to you, and I gave you an adventure to remember, didn't I?"

She kicked him in the leg, but softly. "You idiot. If you loved me, you really should have just told me. And trusted me."

He shook his head. "You really, really think I could have come to you and said, 'Casey, I'm on this winning streak and I think maybe we have to fuck before every time I pitch or I'll lose. So I need you to come to Atlanta so I can do you.' You wouldn't have felt used *then*?"

She chewed on that for a long moment. Too long. The bat boy summoned him back to the field. She thought about it some more.

He's right, she realized. *If he'd said that, she probably* would *have slapped him in the face.*

Then her phone chimed with a text from Missy, just as Casey heard footsteps coming up the tunnel. *Tyler is pitching like a demon, tonight. He just got the side on ten pitches. His total pitch count is only forty-eight right now.*

She looked up as Tyler resumed his place next to her. "Was that the fifth?"

"Yeah," he said tiredly. "The humidity's a killer here, isn't it?" She handed him her water bottle and he took a swig, then handed it back. "Thanks."

"You were right."

"About what?"

"If you'd told me you wanted me to go to Atlanta because of the Streak. I would have been like, 'are you fucking kidding me?' But you lied to get me there."

"No, I didn't. I told you I really wanted someone who loved me there to watch me pitch, remember? Well, that's absolutely true. And when you didn't quibble with me over that description, well, I started to think maybe I could use the L word more often. Maybe work up to actually asking you how you felt, or at least giving you stronger and stronger hints about how I felt. Which I was kind of trying to do, but the time never seemed right."

She put a hand on his shoulder. "But after the game in Chicago, you just couldn't hold it in anymore."

He nodded. "Yeah, basically. I knew I couldn't pull the same thing I did in Atlanta, and Case..." He turned so that he was facing her, his arms resting on his knees. "It wasn't just love at first sight. It's been getting stronger and stronger the more I know you."

"You're sure it isn't just that you keep winning?"

He looked taken aback. "Um, I don't know how to answer that. It's true, I get happier as The Streak gets longer, but...I don't *think* it's that. I think I just love you more and more. Being apart for just a day or two now makes me practically ill. Like I can't eat, can't sleep."

She crossed her arms again. "There's also the fact that I'm totally pissed off at you."

"No, no, no, that started before the fight. Mad Dog was beside himself and pressured me to tell you so that we could get it resolved. He was basically like, 'look, if you love her that much and need her that much, just marry her already and then will you stop with the sad puppy looks?' But I was like, no way, man, this is not some baseball wife. This is an independent woman who, like, has a career and who blew off the last ten guys who proposed to her, or dumped them before they could get to that stage. She's a heartbreaker and I just want to *not* fuck it up and be with her as long as I can. I'll live, I'll be fine, I'm pitching good, so quit bugging me."

"A heartbreaker?" Casey found her hands gripping the water bottle so tight the cap flew off.

"Well, yeah. You told me about all these losers you dumped, didn't you?"

"Yes, but..."

"You don't think those guys were hurt?"

"No, because they were not that into me, either. If they were, then...well..."

He waited until her pause dragged out. "Complete disclosure," he reminded her.

"Well, for one thing, the sex would have been better, because they would have paid a little attention to *me* instead of acting like they won some kind of lottery to get to sleep with me."

He couldn't help laughing at that. "But come on. You're amazing. Don't you think some of them kind of fell for you a little?"

She shrugged. "Well, maybe."

He sighed. "I didn't want to be the next guy on your list of rejects, that's all."

THE HOT STREAK

"Shit, Tyler..." She'd only mentioned the lame-ass losers to him as a contrast, about how different he was, but apparently the message he'd received was more of a warning than she'd intended. "I...I love you, you know. And I really didn't love any of those guys, even though I sometimes tried really hard to."

"Like I tried to love Linda. But it just wasn't all there somehow, and I wasn't really sure of that until I found the real thing. With you. Oh, damn it, that's the bat boy."

Casey watched him go down the tunnel to pitch the sixth inning. She still didn't believe she was the one who'd screwed things up, but she was starting to see how her own hang ups and his had combined together to make a kind of Gordian Knot.

Was there a way to just slice through it?

The security guard she'd seen before came wandering by again. "Hey, you been down here the whole time?" he asked her.

"Um, yeah, why?" She wondered if he was going to try to make her move.

"Just, no radio down here so you might not know. Your boy there is pitching another no-hitter."

"What? Is that even possible?" She stood up in shock.

"Oh, sure. There was one guy, Johnny VanderMeer, in the '30s, pitched two actual no-hitters in back-to-back games. And Hammond didn't actually do it in Chicago, of course." He squinted at her. "Are you the gal he was talking about on TV? Is he coming up here every inning for inspiration from you or something?"

Casey pressed her hands together. "Um, something like that."

"Well, keep it up, I guess. I shouldn't say that, since I work for the Reds, but a no-hitter is a fine thing and, well, it's a lovely story. I hope it all works out for you." He held up his hand as if waving to her, and moved on down the corridor.

Tyler was back before she had a chance to text Missy to ask what was going on.

"You're pitching really fast," she said.

"Is that bad? I'm trying to get back to you quicker," he said. "I'm not striking out guys. Instead I'm letting them hit the ball, and they are mostly hitting them at guys. We piled up a big lead in the first inning, so I keep figuring if I give up a home run, it's no big deal."

"But you're..." She stopped herself before she said the forbidden word. Did he not even realize he was pitching a no-hitter? "You're always pissed off when you give up a homer."

He shrugged. "I'd rather give up a homer and get pulled from the game and get to have this talk with you, uninterrupted, than my usual way of doing things," he said. "But so far no homers, so what can you do?"

"It's all right," she found herself saying. She put her hands on his hips and then leaned up to give him one soft kiss on the cheek. "Let's keep going."

"All right." He held her hands in his. "What do you want to know next?"

Good question. She was amazed to find that her questions about why he'd done all these things she found hurtful seemed to be answered—and the answer seemed to be almost always that he was afraid because he loved her so much. Meanwhile, she'd been afraid to love him in the first place.

She did think of a question, though. "Will you sign the divorce papers as soon as the lawyers can get them to you?"

THE HOT STREAK

"I will. Oh God, Casey, I will."

She found herself hugging him then, her heart aching, but like she'd said to Missy, he was the only one she wanted to soothe that hurt. She couldn't speak. It seemed like neither could he. So they just held each other. She cried a little against his chest. "I'm still really angry at you," she whispered.

"I know," he whispered back. "I'm so sorry."

It felt like far too soon she had to let go so he could go pitch the seventh.

She wiped her tears and texted Missy immediately. *Why didn't you tell me he had a you-know-what going on?*

To which Missy replied: *Don't jinx it.*

Casey thought about that. The guy in Chicago had said some people wouldn't move from their spot in the dugout for fear of breaking the spell somehow. It seemed like maybe she should stay put?

Or was Missy telling her not to jinx The Streak itself?

She sat down on the bucket, suddenly weak in the knees. "Tyler..." It wasn't just her heart that ached, but her whole body. Wasn't that what he described? A need that was painful like thirst or hunger. She shivered despite the heat.

There were questions she still needed to ask, though. About them. About the future. She was standing up waiting for him when he came up the tunnel the next time. She took him by the hands. "Are you going to tell me how you feel and what you want from now on?" she asked. "Even if you're afraid I'll say no or think it's stupid or whatever?"

He thought about it. "I'm going to try to, anyway. I'm not sure I'll always succeed. But what about you? Same?"

She sighed. "Yeah, same. I know how I feel right now, though."

"Angry?"

"Well, yeah, but also I love you, and it's really been painful not being with you." She leaned against him. "And I think I understand a little better now what was going on, so although I'm still pissed off and hurt...I'm a lot less pissed off and hurt."

"Well, that's something," he said, sliding his arms around her.

"Do you believe we have to have sex for you to win games?" she asked.

"Yes," he said. "I know it sounds stupid. But, well, superstition isn't smart. But I can't help what I believe."

"Do you want me to come along with you, and make sure we have sex before every start, so long as The Streak is alive?"

He pulled back just enough to stare into her eyes. "Are you offering to do that?"

"I didn't say that. I asked, do you *want* me to?"

"Yes, God, Casey, absolutely. For the record, though, I don't think it's necessarily strictly speaking *sex* so much as *love*, and well, our expression of love is very, very sexual..."

She raised an eyebrow at him.

"Okay, you're right. That was stretching it a little. Deep down, I think the sex is important."

She nodded and pressed a kiss against his lips as if rewarding him for being so truthful. "Last question for the moment: do you think we need to have sex for you to win this game tonight?"

He thought for a few moments. "I was going to say no, because we're going into the eighth with an eight-run lead, and I know the only reason I'm still in the game is my pitch count is low, but yeah, it seems like a surefire win. But then, that's exactly the kind of thinking that jinxes you."

THE HOT STREAK

"I see," she said. She held him close, wondering if that hardness she felt was his athletic cup or his cock.

CHAPTER TEN

Tyler slid his hand into the hair at the back of Casey's neck. "That fucking bat boy is going to call for me any second now, probably."

Casey leaned up and kissed him, surprised at how quickly a flush seemed to come over her entire body. It had been five days, but it felt like longer. "What inning is it again?"

"The eighth," he said, nibbling at her ear. "I'm about to go pitch the eighth."

So unless he got knocked out of the game in the eighth, they'd get one more chance. "How wet do you think you can make me before then?"

He swore softly. "This isn't exactly the private-est place for that..."

She pulled him down the hallway to the niche she had found earlier, where two pipes ran through from floor to ceiling and she'd left the baseballs on the floor. Behind the pipes, they were more or less out of sight. He pushed her ahead of him, then pulled her against him, her back against his chest.

He ran his hands lightly over her shirt, until her nipples

rose up to meet his touch through the fabric. She pressed back against him, shivering with desire. She'd expected him to be rough, in a hurry, but this was the opposite. On the other hand, it was effective, the teasing touch making her hotter and hungrier than a quick grope would have. *He knows me well.*

His hand slid lower then, as he nibbled at the back of her neck under her hair, seeking out the sensitive spots there. She was so distracted by the teasing of his teeth making her breath catch in her throat that she didn't realize one hand was circling her mound until it had been going on for some time. "Unbutton your jeans," he said to her.

She did, and a moment later she was kissing him over her own shoulder as his hand slid into her panties. "God, I've missed you."

One finger was just starting to slip into her wettest place when the whistle came.

"Three outs, and I'll be back," he breathed in her ear, and he was gone.

Casey leaned against the wall, panting and wondering what Tyler was going to say on ESPN if he pitched a no-hitter.

She stayed in the nook, too flushed to risk being seen just now, wondering if she should text Missy. In the end, she just stayed there, wondering how they were going to manage it in the small space and short amount of time. Should she look for another spot? But then, what if she missed him?

The sound of his cleats hurrying down the hallway sent a thrill through her.

He kissed her then, his arms tight and urgent around her but his mouth soft and coaxing. "I've never needed you more than right now," he whispered.

"Let's do it," she answered.

He pushed her jeans and panties down to her knees and turned her around. She heard the sound of his belt buckle opening behind her, then something hitting the floor. One arm held her close against him while the other hand sought out her wetness again, this time from behind.

"Are you sure this is going to work?"

"It wouldn't if my dick was too small," he said matter-of-factly. With that, he pushed it between her thighs, and she felt the length of him rubbing between her lips. "Oh, jeez, this feels pretty damn good right like this."

"Yeah, for me, too," she said. "But does it count for The Streak?"

"Probably not. Lean forward a little, brace your arms on the wall."

Casey did as he bent his knees more, spreading his feet to lower himself and then pushing up into her. "Holy fuck."

She squeezed him with her inside muscles. "Nah, we'd have to be in a church for that."

They both fell silent then as he began moving in and out of her. Casey picked up his rhythm easily and pushed back into each thrust.

The next thing she felt was his fingers on her clit, too, and she pressed her lips together hard to keep from crying out. How could she be this close already?

"Come on, Casey, want to feel you come, lover. I love you so much, so very much..."

She came around the cock inside her, spasming and squeezing and bucking against him, while he fucked her hard, then harder, trying to reach release himself.

"Oh shit." He stopped suddenly.

"What?" she asked.

The Hot Streak

"The whistle." He was already disengaged from her and buckling his belt. She felt entirely too empty and cold now that his body wasn't pressed against hers. "Well, this is it. Either I do it, or I get sent to the showers. You better get cleaned up, Case."

She turned just in time to see him adjusting his pants one last time and then he was gone, sprinting down the hallway and sliding on his cleats on the concrete until he reached the fake grass part.

On the floor at her feet was his athletic cup.

She knocked on the clubhouse door again, more politely this time, and the attendant let her use the restroom. In here they had the game on TVs in the corners of the room and she managed to get cleaned up and her hair fixed before Tyler had gotten the first batter out. *Yes, good, two more!* she thought.

Then she realized there was no reason for her to stay up here any longer. She ran down the tunnel to the dugout, hanging back just inside the entrance. From here she could see only the upper half of Tyler's body and she couldn't see the batter at all, but it didn't matter. The coach leaning on the steps turned and looked at her, then gave her a little wink and a smile. It made her blush, but she smiled back.

A pinch hitter was announced. She saw Tyler scowl and walk around the back of the mound, picking up the little white sack of rosin there and slamming it back down.

"Come on, Hammond," the coach shouted. "Don't make me go to Rigney again, you pussy bastard! Put this one in the can already!" Then he turned back to Casey. "Um, pardon my French."

"That's okay," she said.

Tyler set himself on the mound. Casey held her breath. She still couldn't see the batter, but she heard the sound of the ball hitting the bat, a loud crack, and the whole stadium seemed to be shaking with people cheering and going wild. The coach was gone. He'd been on his way to the mound before the home run had actually left the ballpark. To Casey's surprise, Tyler was grinning like a fool, though, shaking his head as he handed the ball to the coach.

He practically sprinted off the mound, grabbed her around the waist as he bounded up into the tunnel. "Easy come, easy go!" he said as he hurried her through the clubhouse door.

"Hammond, you no good sonofabitch, what did you think you're..." The clubhouse attendant stopped when he saw Casey. He just threw up his hands and went back into his office.

"Come on," Tyler said. "I've been sent to the showers." He pulled her into the largest shower Casey had ever seen, a huge room with at least ten shower taps, all of them set seven or eight feet high in the wall. Tyler was stripping out of his uniform as fast as he could, and she did the same, taking care to lay her things on a bench.

His cock was rampant and red as a robin's breast, throbbing in her hand as she pressed herself against him.

"What are the chances that Javier gets two quick outs?" he said, walking her backward into the shower area and turning on one of the sunflower-sized shower heads. "If he does, we're going to have an audience real soon."

"I don't care," she said, wrapping one leg around him. "They all know about us anyway."

He kissed her then, this time hard and hungry, and she felt hot water sluice over them like a whole new caress. He hitched her leg up, then the other one, as he pressed her against the wall, his cock rubbing against her right between her lips.

"I'm still wet from before," she said into his ear, as he put her arms around his neck.

He lifted her a little more and she felt the head of his cock nestle against her just there, and then as he lowered her, he filled her. He backed away from the wall a half-step, supporting her weight with his hands under her ass cheeks, then lifted her again. Casey groaned as that ground her clit against him and then he was deep in her once more. She felt the water again and tightened her hold around his neck, helping him to lift her.

"I hope Javier walks the bases loaded," he said into her ear. "Because this is too fucking good to rush."

"Mmmm." They'd never done it standing up before. He felt larger than usual, and she wasn't used to quite so much direct stimulation on her clit while he moved inside her. Much as he didn't want to rush, she would probably come quickly like this as long as he didn't tire.

The muscles in Tyler's arms and back were as hard and straining as his cock itself as he plunged in and out of her again and again. "Oh, yes, more...more..." she urged.

When she came, her voice echoed off the shower walls and he pressed her against the wall again, adding his grunts to her cry, pushing hard.

"Come on, Tyler, finish," she said, thinking of the foul-mouthed coach. "Put it in the can."

His answer was a bellow as he came deep in her, holding himself still and twitching inside her with strong pulses of come.

"Wow," he said, when he could.

"Wow," she agreed.

"Yeah."

"Yeah."

He let her down gently, and then pulled her into the water, kissing her and slicking his hands up and down her skin. "I think we'd better get dressed, because no matter what, there will be TV cameras real soon now."

"Mm-hmm."

He showed her the mountain of clean towels that awaited, wrapping her in one and then toweling her hair and butt until she laughed and forced him to stop. She was just combing her hair with a comb he gave her out of his locker when the door to the clubhouse burst open.

It was Billingham, the assistant general manager. "Oh good, Tyler, Ms. Branigan, you're just who we're looking for. They've got an interview room here and the press would like to meet you both there, instead of cramming in there with the team."

Tyler beamed. "Sure thing! Lead the way." He put an arm around Casey as they followed Billingham out a different door and up a totally different hallway from the one Casey had spent most of the game standing in. They got into an elevator and Billingham pressed a button.

"So," Casey said, with forced casualness. "We held on, right? Game's over?"

Billingham mopped his forehead with a handkerchief, but it was summer humidity and not nerves that had made him

THE HOT STREAK

sweat. "Oh, yes, yes, no problem. Javier had a bit of a rocky time, but with a seven-run lead, even our bullpen isn't that bad."

"Phew, okay, good."

Casey elbowed him in the ribs and he tightened his grip around her shoulders, leading her out of the elevator.

The interview room was packed, and Casey almost held up her hand to block all the bright lights and flashbulbs, then remembered they were actually trying to take her picture, too. She was reminded of those scenes outside courtrooms, except everyone here was so happy. So very happy.

She caught sight of Ken, looking positively misty-eyed, clutching his notepad to his chest. She gave him a little wave as a young man in a Reds polo shirt showed them to two chairs behind a table set with two microphones.

"Okay," said another man in a suit at a podium off to the side. She recognized him as someone who worked for the Robins but she didn't know his name. "We'll take questions." He pointed to someone in the front row of reporters.

It was a woman holding a small tape recorder and a notepad in the same hand. "So, The Streak is alive, and with tonight's win, the Robins are in serious contention for a playoff spot. How do you feel about that, Tyler?"

"Oh my God, it's awesome. That's the thing about The Streak, of course. It's kind of cool, I know, but the more important thing is that we're winning games. Not just me, but the whole team. If I can keep pitching well, it means we can't get into any bad losing streaks. So that's awesome. I really hope it keeps up. The winning, I mean, not The Streak necessarily, because it'd be much more important to me that we win the World Series than I got some new line in the record books."

The guy running the show pointed to another reporter, a balding man with glasses. "Yes, so, after your last start, which was almost a no-hitter, and then this one with the same thing, Tyler Hammond, are you jinxed?"

"What?" Tyler laughed and took Casey's hand in his. "Are you kidding me? I am so incredibly lucky. I am the luckiest man in the world!" Everyone laughed at that and Casey wondered why that was so funny. Tyler looked a little taken aback, too, but he rolled with it. "This is Casey, everybody. She's the one I talked about last post-game. I fell in love with her the day I plunked Campbell and we had that big dust-up, you remember? And I left early after visiting the press box? Everyone thought it was because I couldn't stand to see the bullpen lose another game for me? Well, it was actually that Casey here was in the stands and I skipped out early to take her on a date. And well, you know the rest of the story. We've been dating ever since, and I've been winning ever since."

"Wait a second, just trying to get the quote straight," yelled a voice from the back. Casey couldn't quite see the reporter because of the lights. "So you're saying that the power of love is what's making you pitch so good?"

"Well," Tyler joked, "Casey here can attest that it ain't steroids." He made a motion with his fingers like something shrinking. "But seriously, yes. When she's there, it's like I feel amazing. Like I can do anything. Or almost anything, since I haven't quite managed the no-hitter yet."

Ken spoke up next. "My question's for Casey. So, what's your take on The Streak? Tyler here seems to believe you need to be at the ballpark to keep the luck going."

Casey leaned close to the microphone, squeezing Tyler's hand. "All I can really say is that, you know, it's been a streak for me, too. I've tried Internet dating, speed dating, blind dates, you name it, and Tyler is the first guy I've found in years that I've been with this long. And I want to be with him for a long time to come. For me, I hope this streak is a lot longer than a baseball season."

The flashbulbs were blinding as Tyler pulled her into a prolonged kiss.

The next few weeks were a whirlwind for Casey. As August came to a close, Tyler won three more starts in a row, and the story just kept getting bigger and bigger. Casey did more interviews, took a leave of absence from work, and threw herself into selling the cookbook with the wives when it arrived. Each game the wives would set up a little stand on the concourse to sell the cookbook and also run a silent auction of memorabilia signed by the players. Casey was in charge of getting things from Tyler as each woman was in charge of getting things from her guy. Tyler's autographs were going for ridiculous amounts, thanks to The Streak.

The day of Tyler's eighteenth start since they had met fell on a Sunday, and the game was chosen to be the ESPN Sunday Night game of the week. A producer from ESPN called Casey to ask if she would mind coming on the broadcast in the fifth inning to talk about The Streak. She readily agreed.

She and Missy sat in their usual seats, about ten rows back from the dugout. Missy had made sure her auburn hair color job was absolutely perfect because, she said, she knew they'd be on television a lot that night. Casey had at least worn a nice jacket and blouse and put on just a little makeup so she wouldn't look too washed out if they actually showed her on the broadcast.

Tyler was pitching well, but the Robins were only leading by one run in the fourth when a production assistant came down to get Casey and bring her up to the broadcast booth. He looked like he was about eighteen, in a button-down shirt and loafers. "Miss Branigan? John and Joe are ready for you now. If you would turn your cell phone off?"

"Here," she said, putting her phone into her purse and handing it to Missy. "See you in a bit." She followed the kid up the aisle, then up the next aisle to the very top of the main seating section where there was a side door she'd never really noticed before. He pulled it open and they went up only half a flight of stairs and into the back of a production booth. "I never realized this was here."

"Yeah, we're not as high up as you think," the kid said. "Just above the backstop screen, which means foul balls can still fly into the booth, though." He opened another door and they went into the actual broadcast booth. Two announcers in suits were there, one black, one white, and they shook Casey's hand while they kept talking, narrating the game live. She had already forgotten which one was John and which was Joe. The kid fitted her with a wireless microphone and she was silent while he did.

"It's okay, you can talk," he said quietly. "It's not on yet."

"Oh, okay."

"Just talk normally. You don't have to act like you're talking into a microphone or anything." He pinned it to her lapel. "You don't have to be facing it exactly or anything. You can move your head normally."

"Thanks."

THE HOT STREAK

"Okay, they're ready for you."

He steered Casey until she was standing between the two announcers and they shook her hand again, this time talking to her directly.

"And we have, joining us in the booth tonight, Casey Branigan," said the first, mellifluous-voiced announcer. "She has become a sort of *cause celebre* in the sports world, and I guess beyond the sports world, because of her story. Casey, welcome."

"Thanks for having me," she said. "It's been kind of a magical mystery tour since I met Tyler."

The other announcer spoke. "Oh, you get points for making a Beatles reference! Doesn't she, John? But yes, I know you've told the story before, but for those who missed it, tell us how you met Tyler Hammond." But he held up a hand so she wouldn't speak yet.

"Hammond has just finished his warm-up pitches for this inning and is getting ready to face the first batter of the inning, third baseman Matt Henson," said John.

They motioned for her to speak then. "I met him at my day job," she said. "You remember that ad campaign a while back that had him in a suit of armor?"

"Was it for Gillette?" Joe asked, but the kid was waving his arms. *Probably trying to get them not to mention any brand names that hadn't paid for a sponsorship*, Casey thought.

"Um, someone like that," she said.

"And Henson takes a strike on the outside corner," John said, motioning to her to continue.

"Well, it was on that photo shoot that we met, and he asked if I'd go to the game to see him pitch that night, and I did, and

I really fell in love with him that night, though it took me a while to admit it."

"And strike two, that one looked right down the middle. I don't know what Henson was waiting for. That was a good pitch to hit."

"Maybe he was guessing curve ball?" Joe opined.

"Maybe, Joe. Looks like maybe catcher John Madison was expecting the curve, too, as he's just gone out to the mound to talk things over with Hammond. So, Casey, he won that night and he's won every game since."

"That's right, John," she said. "If he wins tonight, he'll set a new record for straight starts with a winning decision." She'd practiced that phrase a hundred times, since it seemed important to get it right.

"Of course, the record is held by Carl Hubbell, who set a streak of twenty-four wins in the '36-'37 season. But that was twenty-four wins including some as a starting pitcher, some as a relief pitcher, and he also had some no decisions in there." John chuckled. "And Hammond also almost put himself in the company of another pitcher from the 1930s, Johnny Vander-Meer."

"Oh! The guy who pitched the two no-hitters in a row," Casey said suddenly, remembering what the security guard in Cincinnati had told her.

"That's right!" Joe sounded impressed. "You really know your baseball history, Casey, which is pretty neat considering that you're now a part of it."

"That's right," John continued. "The conference on the mound is over, and Henson is back in the box. Hammond kicks and deals...strike three! He's out of there! But yes, Casey, during Hubbell's streak he had seventeen in a row that were all starts and with no intervening no-decisions. So that stood as the record until last week, when Tyler Hammond tied it. So at the very least, Hammond, with you as his pitching muse, are in the record books already. Now here comes shortstop Donald Franco to the plate."

"Oh, I remember him, too," Casey said. The skinny rookie that Tyler and Mad Dog had schooled with wild pitches much earlier in the season.

"That's right," John said. "That was an ESPN Sunday Night game too and well, Casey, you know better than anyone that Tyler Hammond is sometimes prone to some hijinks. I wonder if there's any bad blood between Franco and him over that?"

"I think Tyler sent Franco a bottle of champagne, actually," she said. "Since that was his way of saying 'welcome to the Major League.'"

"Well, now, Franco is talking to the umpire, and gesticulating toward the mound," John said. "What do you make of that, Joe?"

"Well, he looks a bit upset, John. He's pointing at Hammond and stomping his foot a little. Hammond hasn't even thrown a pitch yet, so I don't know what he's arguing about."

"Well, and now it seems the umpire and the catcher, the veteran John Madison, are going partway to the mound and asking to talk to Tyler. And here comes the manager, wanting to know what's going on..."

"Oh, I see. Franco's pointing to his ear now." Joe tugged on his own ear. "I bet he's saying Tyler's got to take his earring off. We've seen this a bunch of times in the past few years. The batter has the right to ask for jewelry to be removed if it's distracting to him. Usually you only see that on a bright, sunny day, but it does look like that's what he's doing."

Down on the field, Tyler was doing something to his ear. Casey stared. Had Tyler gotten an earring before the game? Missy had said the team was probably going to do something together along the lines of all cutting their hair, a bonding thing for the stretch run to the playoffs. Had they all gotten their ears pierced? Casey tried to imagine them all in line at a jewelry cart in Faneuil Hall.

"Well," John said, "it seems like they're making him remove something, anyway. But now he's refusing to give it to Madison or the umpire."

"I don't blame him," said Joe. "That's probably a ten-thousand-dollar diamond or something he's got on there. No wonder it was flashing in Franco's eyes."

The producer picked up the phone and then said something to Joe. "We just got a call from the security guard down at field level saying that Tyler Hammond says he'll only give it to you, Casey."

"Are we going to go to commercial?"

Their voices receded as the production assistant who had brought her to the studio helped her back down the same aisle. For a moment, she wondered why he was following her when she realized she was still wearing the microphone and he must either have wanted it back, or maybe once this was all resolved, they were going to continue the interview. After all, there were still two more outs to go in the inning.

She saw Travis was the security guard by the field, waving her down to the edge of the dugout with a huge smile on his face. Tyler came jogging to the side of the field to meet her, the umpire, Mad Dog, Franco, and a bunch of other people trailing behind him.

Tyler was holding the earring in his glove, with his free hand over it, as if he were afraid it was going to blow away in the wind. "Casey?" he asked.

"Yeah?" She looked at him. He had the oddest look in his eyes. "Everything okay, Tyler?"

"Um, I hope so." He pulled something gold with an incredibly bright diamond on it out of his glove, then handed the glove to Mad Dog. "Casey Branigan, I have something to ask you." He looked up at her, his eyes huge and wide as he pushed the brim of his cap back a little.

She had only half a second to think, *what?* before he asked her the question.

He dropped to one knee at the base of the wall and held the diamond up. "Casey Branigan, will you marry me?"

"Oh my God, Tyler, I..." For some reason something Missy had said to her months ago popped into her head, about the pitcher being the center of attention of fifty thousand people, and about how Tyler in particular had no qualms about making the entire game stop and wait for him. Fifty thousand people here. And how many millions watching at home.

She dared a glance at the PA standing nervously by. "Is this thing on?" She touched the microphone, the enormity of the set-up for it all just beginning to dawn on her. The kid gave half a nod.

"Tyler Hammond," she said, taking his hands which still held the ring, "yes. The streak that matters most to me is a lot longer than a baseball season, or a baseball career."

He squeezed her hand, then slipped the ring onto her finger and stood up to hug her, then pulled her over the wall as he swung her around. "She said yes! She said yes!" he shouted as he spun in a circle, Casey's legs flying out as he did so.

When he set her on her feet, the entire crowd was standing and applauding, and then he kissed her, just a quick one this time, and then held up her hand like a prize fighter's. "Wave to the crowd!" he urged her. She did as she made her way back to the stands and Travis helped her back over the wall into the aisle, then hugged her himself.

She pulled the microphone off and handed it to the poor PA who was looking nervous. "Here you go," she said. "Sorry, I think your station got enough of me for one day." He fled back up the aisle just as Missy was coming to hug her, too, and Lila Gutierrez, and even Shayna and Michaela.

It was a few minutes before she got back into her actual seat, by which time Tyler had retired both Franco and the batter after him, and the Robins' first batter had already gotten a hit. Missy made her hold up the ring so it sparkled in the stadium lights. "Damn, that's pretty," she said.

"It is," Casey agreed.

"Now, here, your purse has been vibrating like crazy." Missy handed her the purse and Casey dug her phone out.

She had voice mail and text messages from her mother, her brother, her boss, Kim, Ken, and a half-dozen other numbers she didn't even recognize. She turned the phone off. "I'll call them back later. Right now, there's four innings to go."

"Damn straight," Missy said, crossing her ankles and settling back in her seat.

"Campbell's going to hit a home run," Casey said.

"You think?"

"Yeah. So when should we have the wedding?"

"If you want soon, your best bet is in January, or maybe

the first week of February. Pitchers and catchers report to spring training usually on February fourteenth."

"Valentine's Day?"

"Yep. Go figure." Missy clapped her hands. "Here comes Campbell now. So Tyler must have totally put Franco up to that, don't you think?"

Casey looked around the ballpark, so brightly lit and full of happy people. It had reminded her of the circus that first day and it still did. "He must have. And the ESPN guys. And Mad Dog knew, obviously."

"Oh yeah, I think he actually had the ring on him and slipped it to Tyler. I'll have to ask him later."

"Yeah. And Travis totally knew, too. He was grinning like a fool when he saw me, I just didn't know why at first." She smiled. "Now Ken is finally out of the doghouse for good. He told me last week he wants to write a book about us, about me and Tyler. He says he's got a publisher interested, but they really only want it if The Streak breaks the record. But that if he does, and if they win the World Series this year, then they are all over it."

The crowd gasped as Campbell clobbered a ball but it went foul. "Come on, you big palooka," Casey said under her breath. "I know Tyler will want Mad Dog to be the best man, but you think Campbell will be a good groomsman?"

Missy thought about it for half a second. "Yes."

"You're going to be my maid of honor, right? Or, matron of honor, I guess it would be? God, I don't know these things," Casey groaned.

"You betcha," Missy said with a grin. "Didn't your parents say they wanted to go to Aruba for Christmas? We could totally do it down there and fly everyone in, you know. White sand, beach wedding. That's of course if you want to get it done in the off season. There's always the ballpark wedding, too, you know, where all your teammates hold up bats to make the aisle and you walk from the mound to the plate and get married at home plate."

Casey thought about that for all of half a second. "Hmm. It has some charm, but Aruba sounds better. Where did you get married?"

"In Montgomery, Alabama, where he was playing minor league ball for almost no money," Missy said. "Home plate was all we could afford. I'll show you the pictures some time. It was really nice and charming, but...yeah. Aruba."

And suddenly there was a loud crack and Casey found herself jumping to her feet along with the rest of the crowd. It meant a two-run homer, a nice three-run lead for Tyler, and a new record nearly guaranteed. But at that moment, all Casey felt was pure excitement and wonder as she watched that tiny ball sail away into the black velvet of the night, pushed higher and higher by fifty thousand cheers.

THE END

ACKNOWLEDGMENTS

Special thanks to Ed Hooper, Matthew B. Tepper, and Michael Cavallo, who helped me research the consecutive win streak records for pitchers. All of the facts about Carl Hubbell and Johnny VanderMeer are real. (The rest of the ballplayers mentioned, well, except for Babe Ruth, Cy Young, and Tommy John, are all inventions of my own.) I don't know if I'm the first member of the Society for American Baseball Research (SABR) to write a baseball romance novel, but I thank the organization profusely for their support.

Thanks to Jean Roberta, Patrick Weekes, and Claudia Mastroianni, who all provided feedback on the first draft.

They say every romance novel has some elements of wish fulfillment, and for me, a huge baseball fan living in Boston, this book has some elements of that, for sure. Putting a National League team here is a pure fantasy of mine, too.

About the Author

Cecilia Tan is the award-winning author of numerous works of romance and erotica, not to mention baseball nonfiction. Her novel *Slow Surrender* won the RT Reviewers Choice Award for Erotic Romance. Her other romances include *Mind Games,* the Struck by Lightning series, and the Magic University series. Tan's erotic short stories have been collected in the books *Black Feathers, White Flames, Edge Plays,* and *Telepaths Don't Need Safewords* and she has also edited close to a hundred erotica anthologies for various publishers including Circlet Press, the publishing house she founded in 1992. She lives in the Boston area with her partner corwin and three cats.

The 50 Greatest Red Sox Games
by Cecilia Tan and Bill Nowlin

Every Red Sox fan cherishes memories of great games that will never be forgotten, and wonders what it would have been like to be in the park for other outstanding moments from the team's checkered past. Were you there when Roger Clemens notched his first 20-strikeout game? Where were you on that incredible day—October 27, 2004—when the curse was shattered?

Covering the history of the Boston Red Sox, The 50 Greatest Red Sox Games lets you relive the very best (and worst) moments dating back to 1903. From history-making plays to historic achievements, Cecilia Tan and Bill Nowlin recreate the suspense, excitement, and drama of every game on the list. Drawing on in-depth research, personal player interviews, and newspaper and magazine accounts of the day, they recreate the action on the field and the history surrounding it.

The Circlet Treasury of
Lesbian Erotic Science Fiction
edited by Cecilia Tan

In these pages women writers turn their vivid imaginations to faraway planets, erotic futures, and sensual fairytales, to celebrate sexuality and explore what it means to be a woman who loves women. In these stories, women seek their pleasure through magic, from goddesses, in enchanted forests, and with fairy women. Taking desire out of our modern-day political context, and letting imagination run free, these writers create fantasies like no other. This outstanding collection of lesbian erotic science fiction and fantasy was originally published as two anthologies, *Worlds of Women* and *Stars Inside Her.*